"I'm going to live here."

His answer made no sense. "What do you mean? Along the river?"

"No." He bit at his lip and took a deep breath. "I'm sorry. I had no idea you were Savannah Carmichael. I didn't know any of the Carmichaels were still alive."

Her heart began to pound in fear. She knew she was about to receive news that threatened everything she held dear. "What are you trying to tell me?"

He exhaled. "I bought Cottonwood yesterday at the court-house in Selma."

She heard the words, but she couldn't believe it. A stabbing pain ripped at her heart. "You can't have Cottonwood," she cried. "It belongs to me."

SANDRA ROBBINS and her husband live in the small college town where she grew up. Until a few years ago she was working as an elementary school principal, but God opened the door for her to become a full-time writer. Without the help of her wonderful husband, four children, and five grandchildren who have supported her dreams for many years, it would be impossible to write. As a child, Sandra accepted Jesus as her Savior and has depended on Him to guide her throughout her life. It is her prayer that God will use her words to plant seeds of hope in the lives of her readers. To find out more about Sandra and her books, go to her Web site at http://sandrarobbins.net.

The Columns
of Cottonwood

Sandra Robbins

Heartsong Presents

To Jay, Megan, Katie, Sydney, and Kylie, my wonderful grandchildren. I pray you will always look to God for direction in your lives. No matter where you go and what you pursue in life, you can be assured that He is watching over you.

A note from the Author:
I love to hear from my readers! You may correspond with me by writing:

Sandra Robbins
Author Relations
PO Box 721
Uhrichsville, OH 44683

ISBN 978-1-60260-486-5

THE COLUMNS OF COTTONWOOD

one

A low, musical rumble like distant thunder drifted through the afternoon quiet. Savannah Carmichael paused before climbing into the buggy outside her aunt's house and listened. The familiar sound floated from the direction of the river.

The horse hitched to the buggy jerked up his head and whinnied at the deep-pitched drone. Jasper Green, her aunt's handyman, stroked the horse's back and grinned. "There's the whistle. The *Liberty Queen* done docked. I 'spect we's be seein' lots of folks flockin' to town."

Savannah nodded and stepped into the buggy. "I'm sure the merchants will be glad to see the passengers come ashore. They always spend a lot of money."

Excitement washed over her as it did each time she heard a steamboat arrive. The *Montgomery Belle*, the *Carrie Davis*, the *Liberty Queen*, the *Alabama Maiden*—she knew them all and recognized their distinct whistles.

Today she'd get to see the *Liberty Queen*, because her route would take her by the landing. She never tired of watching the passengers from the big paddle wheelers walk from the boat up the hill to the small port town of Willow Bend, Alabama. Her mind would whirl with all sorts of visions as she imagined herself a passenger in unfamiliar locations and disembarking with enough money to buy whatever her heart desired.

She smiled. "Wouldn't it be wonderful to sail away on a steamboat and leave all our problems behind?"

Jasper pushed his tattered straw hat back and gazed up at her. "You'd just have to come back sometime, Miss 'Vanna. Besides, it takes money to ride boats, and I doan think we's seen much of that 'round here lately."

She laughed, smoothed her long skirt, and reached for the reins Jasper held. "Not since the war at least. But one day that will all change, Jasper. I just know it will."

"Yas'm. That's what you been sayin' for a long time now, but I ain't seen no taxes being paid."

A sigh rippled through her body. "No, not yet, but I have faith God's going to provide us with the money somehow."

Jasper shook his head. "I hope you right." He patted the horse's flank and glanced up. "Miss 'Vanna, why doan you let me drive you today? It jest ain't fit'n for a lady to be drivin' by herself. I be more'n glad to go wit' you."

Savannah let her gaze wander over Jasper, and her heart warmed at the kindness in his face. He had been given to Aunt Jane by her father as a wedding present, and Jasper had dedicated his life to taking care of his mistress. Even when he was granted his freedom, he couldn't bring himself to leave.

Now with her parents dead, he was taking care of her, too. Savannah leaned out the side of the buggy and patted Jasper's shoulder. "You're so good to us, Jasper, but I'll be fine. I should be back long before supper."

Jasper frowned and backed away from the buggy. "Be careful when you goes down Main Street. Them folks gittin' off dat boat doan pay no 'tention to where they's goin'."

Savannah laughed and tightened her grip on the reins. "I know what you mean. I saw a man and woman step right in front of a wagon the last time the *Maiden* docked."

"You jest keep a keen eye out for 'em."

"I will." Savannah cast a glance back toward the house. "I left Aunt Jane resting. I don't think she's feeling well today. Will you check on her after a while?"

Jasper's eyes clouded with concern at the mention of his mistress. "Yas'm. I 'spect I best go do that right now."

Savannah flicked the reins and headed down the street toward the docks. With any luck, passengers would still be getting off, and she would get a look at the people traveling the Alabama River in luxury.

The August sun bore down on her as she rode down the dirt street that ran in front of Aunt Jane's house. Dust, stirred by the horse's hooves and the buggy, boiled up around her. The last three months had been hotter than usual, and she welcomed the coming of fall's cooler temperatures.

Of course there was no place she'd rather live than in the Black Belt of Alabama, so named because of the rich, black soil that extended along the Alabama River. She might dream of traveling on one of the big paddle wheelers that stopped at Willow Bend, but she would always be drawn to the canebrakes and farmland that lay along the twisting river.

Her lifestyle had certainly changed when the war began. The once lush fields of Cottonwood had returned to the wild when most of the slaves left, and money had been nonexistent. In the years following the war, her father had been content to sit on the veranda and dream about the past, but that, too, came to an end two years ago when a fire took the house and her parents' lives. Now at twenty years of age, all she had was a deserted plantation with years of unpaid back taxes, but she didn't worry about that. No Southern gentlemen would buy another's land for the back taxes. It was an unspoken code of conduct.

She thought of Aunt Jane's two-story whitewashed house where she'd lived since the death of her parents and how different it was from what she'd known all her life. It had come to be home, but it would never be Cottonwood. That's where her heart lay and where her parents were buried.

At the end of the street, Savannah guided the horse through a left turn and headed for the docks. As she approached the landing, she glanced toward the river and the boat moored at the shore. Its white sides glittered in the sun, and crew members hurried along the three decks. Smoke still poured from the two tall stacks near the front as dockworkers loaded waiting goods aboard for shipment to upriver ports.

In the midst of the bustling activity, passengers walked across the gangplank and headed up the hill. In front of her, people already strolled across the street. One woman held a white ruffled parasol over her head to shade her face from the hot sun. As Savannah drew closer, she could see the delicate lace that covered the umbrella.

She squinted and tried to get a better look at the woman. Rows of ruffles draped the back of her blue traveling dress, and its hem swept across the dusty street.

Lost in thought about the elegant lady, Savannah pulled her gaze away and screamed in terror at the sight of her horse bearing down on a man in the middle of the street. He looked around in surprise and jumped back out of the path of the buggy.

The horse, sensing danger, reared on its hind legs as she tugged on the reins with all her might. In the same instant, the man leaped forward and grabbed the horse's harness. He struggled with the animal while she continued to pull on the reins. After a few tense moments, the horse quieted.

When he was able to release his hold on the harness, the

man stepped to the side of the buggy and stared up at her. A frown lined his face. "Are you all right, miss?"

Savannah stared into eyes the color of ink. They widened for a moment as she gazed down at him, and she almost gasped aloud at the murky depth she sensed in his gaze. Not only were his eyes dark, but so was the hair sticking out from under his felt bowler. His bronzed skin bore evidence of long hours outdoors, but his calloused hands caught her attention. He might be traveling in luxury, but he wasn't one of the idle rich. This man was used to hard work.

She shook her head to clear her thoughts. "I'm fine, but what about you? I'm so sorry. I didn't see you."

He smiled, and his white teeth offered a stark contrast to his dark features. "It was my fault. I wasn't watching where I was going. I'm sorry to cause you trouble."

She glanced at the steamboat. "Are you a passenger?"

He nodded. "I was, but Willow Bend is my destination."

Savannah tilted her head and studied the man. Willow Bend was just a stopover on the upriver or downriver routes. It wasn't anyone's destination. "Are you visiting someone?"

He chuckled. "No. I've bought some land, and I'm settling here."

She glanced past him to the boat. "Is your family traveling with you?"

He shook his head. "I have no family." His gaze traveled over the stores along the street. "Maybe you can help me. I need to rent a horse. Where is the livery stable?"

She pointed in the direction she'd just come. "Go down this street, and you'll see it on the left."

He tipped his hat and backed away from the buggy. "Thank you. Maybe we'll meet again."

The horse snorted and pawed at the ground. She wrapped

the reins around her hands. "I'd better be going. I hope you like living at Willow Bend."

His eyes sparkled. "I'm sure I will."

Savannah snapped the reins across the horse's back. As the buggy surged forward, she chuckled. No family meant he didn't have a wife. The presence of a new eligible bachelor in town should stir the local female interest. She could hardly wait until Sunday to see if he showed up at church.

&

Dante Rinaldi stood in the middle of the street and watched the buggy disappear in the distance. He'd never seen anyone as beautiful as the young woman he'd just encountered. Her blond hair shimmered in the summer sun, and her blue eyes reminded him of the water off the Gulf Coast.

He wondered how old she was. Perhaps twenty but no more. She was at least ten years younger than he. Her beauty reminded him of what his life had lacked since his parents' deaths sixteen years ago. Each waking moment had been dedicated to work and saving his money for the day he would buy his own land. He'd never had time for love, and now he feared it was too late. He might never find what his parents had treasured.

However, all his years of hard work had paid off, and even better than he thought. He closed his eyes for a moment and thought back to the trip from Mobile to Montgomery before the war, when he'd first seen the plantation homes along the bluff near Willow Bend. One had caught his attention, and it was the memory of the grand house and its columns that had motivated him to work even harder.

Never in his wildest dreams had he dared hope the mansion and its land could be his. Now it was. Or what was left of it. Someday the land would be the great plantation it had once been, and the house would be restored and even larger than before. All it would take was hard labor, and he knew how to do that.

With a smile on his face, he turned in the direction the young lady had pointed. The first thing he had to do was rent a horse and go take a look at his land.

❧

An hour later, Dante pulled the horse to a stop at the edge of what had once been a well-manicured lawn that rolled down the steep bluff in front of an imposing mansion. Now with the area overgrown with thick weeds and brambles, the view of the river was almost blocked.

Underneath him the horse twitched with restlessness, and he leaned forward to pat her neck and whisper in her ear. His gaze returned to the eight, smoke-streaked columns that towered above him, the only remnants that remained of the great house. The clerk at the courthouse had told him there had originally been thirty-two of the forty-five-foot Corinthian columns lining the four sides of the home. All but the eight front ones had been destroyed in the fire that consumed the house.

Dante closed his eyes, and for a moment he envisioned the house as it was when he first glimpsed it from the river. Gone now was the mansion with its balconies that circled the house. He remembered a young girl standing on the second floor beside one of the columns and waving to the passengers on the boat. Perhaps she died in the fire that took the lives of the owner and his wife.

"Evenin', suh. You needs some he'p?"

The quiet drawl surprised Dante, and he swiveled in the saddle. A man with skin the color of chocolate stood next to one of the columns. His fixed stare told Dante the man harbored a protective attitude toward his surroundings.

Dante dismounted and tied the horse to a birch tree still standing in the yard. He walked toward the man, who hadn't moved, and extended his hand. "I'm Dante Rinaldi. I just bought this land."

The man's eyebrows arched, and he licked at his lips. "You done bought Cottonwood?"

Dante nodded. "That's right. The plantation's mine, all one thousand acres of it." The man still hadn't taken his hand, and Dante let his arm dangle to his side. "Do you live around here?"

A look of fear crossed the man's face, and he glanced over his shoulder. "Me and my woman, Mamie, we lives in the same cabin we al'ays had when Mistuh Vance be here."

Dante frowned. "You didn't leave when you were given your freedom?"

The man shook his head. "No use us a-doin' that. We doan have no place else. So we stayed and he'ped out."

"But what about after the owner died?"

He shrugged. "Nobody tole us to leave." His lips trembled. "I 'spect you be a-wantin' us gone now, though."

Dante looked at the muscles bulging under the man's tattered shirt and recognized strength in his arms and shoulders. But it was the sadness in his eyes at the thought of leaving his home that touched Dante's heart.

"Tell you what," Dante said. "I'm going to be needing workers here. Would you consider staying on as a tenant farmer? We could work the land together on shares, and you could have a plot of ground to grow your food and keep some animals. Maybe a cow or two and some hogs."

The man's mouth gaped open. "I sho' would like that, and I be a good worker for you. I got me two boys, and they strong.

My Mamie, she works hard, too."

Dante held out his hand again. "Then why don't we shake on it, and we'll work out the details later, Mr. . . . I don't think you ever told me your name."

Unable to pull his stare from Dante's hand, the man reached out and grasped the outstretched fingers. "Saul Clark, suh."

"Well, Saul, I'm looking forward to working with you. Where's your cabin?"

Saul pointed over his shoulder. "Out yonder in the old quarters. We still be in the one we al'ays lived in."

"Is there an empty one I can stay in?"

Saul's eyes widened. "Suh, you gwine live in slave quarters?"

Dante laughed. "It doesn't look like there's any other shelter around here. One of the cabins will be fine until we can build something better for both of us."

Dante didn't think Saul's eyes could get any bigger, but they did. "Both of us? You mean we gwine build somethin' for me and Mamie, too?"

"Of course. The land has plenty of timber on it. We might as well put it to good use."

Saul's legs twitched, and Dante thought he might jump up and down. "I's got to go tell Mamie the good Lawd done answered our prayers."

Dante laughed. "You do that. I want to look around a bit, and then I'll come on to your cabin."

Saul turned and ran, leaving Dante smiling at the retreating figure. He'd thanked the Lord, too, when he found out he could purchase Cottonwood for the back taxes, but he didn't think his happiness could start to compare with what he'd seen on Saul's face.

Dante turned and looked back toward the river. The first

thing he wanted to do was clear out the saplings and all the growth that had sprung up. He wanted the view open so he could sit outside on quiet nights and watch the Alabama River roll by his land.

Now he wanted to walk across the soil he had purchased. Maybe then he'd really believe his dream had come true.

He glanced to the right, and to his surprise he spied a path that ran along the edge of the bluff. Vegetation didn't cover the lane, giving it a traveled appearance. He strode toward it and headed along the bluff on the path.

After walking about two hundred yards, the river swung to the left, and the path veered away from the water. As he rounded the bend of the trail, he stopped in surprise at the sight of a buggy ahead, the horse tied to a tree. Treading as lightly as possible, he eased around the buggy and stopped in astonishment at the sight of a white fence surrounding a small cemetery. Tall water oaks shaded the area where five or six tombstones protruded from the ground.

A woman knelt between two of the graves. She leaned forward, and he could hear her whispered voice. He strained to understand the words, but they were too soft.

"Excuse me," he called out.

The woman sprang to her feet and whirled to face him. Fear etched her face.

Dante's breath gushed from his body as if he'd just been kicked in the stomach. The woman facing him was the one who'd almost run him down in Willow Bend.

two

Savannah could hardly believe her eyes. The stranger she'd encountered in town had followed her. Now she was at his mercy.

She took a step back. "Leave me alone, or I'll cry for help."

The man's lips twitched. "You may have to holler really loud. Saul went back to his cabin."

She looked around for an escape route, but the man blocked her path. "You know Saul?"

"Yes." He moved closer. "Please don't be afraid. You surprised me as much as I did you." He smiled, and in that gesture she realized he meant her no harm. She relaxed.

"My name is Dante Rinaldi. I think we met earlier in town."

She nodded. "Yes, we did. Did you follow me here?"

His lips parted, and a deep laugh rumbled from his throat. "No. I was walking along the river. What are you doing here?"

She felt more at ease, so she pointed to the tombstones. "I'm visiting my parents' graves."

His eyes clouded, and he frowned. "Your parents?"

"Yes. I'm Savannah Carmichael. My parents, Vance and Amelia, are buried here."

"Your parents were the owners of Cottonwood?" Surprise laced the words.

She walked through the gate of the white fence surrounding the cemetery and latched it. "The house burned two years ago. My parents died in the fire, but I was able to escape by sliding down one of the columns from the second-floor balcony." She stopped in front of the man. "Did you say your name is Rinaldi?"

He swallowed. "Yes."

She tilted her head to one side. "That's an unusual name."

"I'm Italian."

She smiled. "You don't speak with an accent. Have you lived in America long?"

He nodded. "All my life. My parents came to this country before I was born. I grew up in the Mobile area." His dark eyes seemed to bore into her.

"When I almost ran you over, I thought you told me you had no family."

He shook his head. "I don't. My parents died of yellow fever."

She sighed. "I'm sorry. We have yellow fever outbreaks quite often, too."

"So I've heard."

She started to question him further about his reasons for choosing Willow Bend but decided she'd already been too inquisitive. "I'm sorry to be asking so many questions. I'm sure you'll like living here. You'll have to come to church next Sunday and meet all the people who live around here."

"I'd like that." His gaze shifted away from her, and she noticed a drop of perspiration trickle down his cheek.

A warning floated somewhere in the recesses of her mind. Why was he here on her land? She should have questioned him more before she lapsed into conversation with him.

She frowned and gazed up at him. "You haven't told me where you're going to live."

He pulled a handkerchief from his pocket and dabbed at the perspiration that now seemed to be popping out all over his face. "I'm going to live here."

His answer made no sense. "What do you mean? Along the river?"

"No." He bit at his lip and took a deep breath. "I'm sorry. I had no idea you were Savannah Carmichael. I didn't know any of the Carmichaels were still alive."

Her heart began to pound in fear. She knew she was about to receive news that threatened everything she held dear. "What are you trying to tell me?"

He exhaled. "I bought Cottonwood yesterday at the courthouse in Selma."

She heard the words, but she couldn't believe it. A stabbing pain ripped at her heart. "You can't have Cottonwood," she cried. "It belongs to me."

"The taxes haven't been paid in years. The county had the right to sell it." Sympathy lined his face, but she refused to acknowledge it.

She doubled her fists and advanced on him. "But I was going to pay the taxes and come back here to live. You can't do this to me."

He backed away. "I'm sorry, Miss Carmichael. I didn't mean to cause you any hurt, but Cottonwood now belongs to me."

She raised her hand to strike him, but she hesitated. Violence had never solved anything. She should know that after seeing what the war had done to her parents and their plantation. She stepped back and glared. "Well, you can't have it. It's supposed to pass to my heirs. Not some Italian carpetbagger who takes advantage of other people's misfortunes."

His dark eyes flashed. "I'm not a carpetbagger. I've worked for years to get enough money to buy some land. Now I have it. I'm sorry for your problems, but they aren't of my making."

Her chest heaved as she turned, climbed into the buggy, and grabbed the reins. "This isn't the end, Mr. Rinaldi. I intend to get Cottonwood back."

He reached out and grabbed the horse's reins as he had done earlier in town. "Until you do, Miss Carmichael, please feel free to visit your parents' graves anytime you want. Cottonwood will always welcome your visit."

She bit back the retort hovering on the tip of her tongue, snapped the reins, and turned the buggy in a circle. With a heavy heart, she guided the horse down the path toward the ruins of her home.

At that moment, the whistle of the *Liberty Queen* rumbled from the river. She glanced at the sleek paddle wheeler churning its way through the winding channel. She hoped the cargo headed to the upriver ports would be more welcome than what the steamboat had delivered to her. She'd convinced herself this day would never come. Now it had, and the last remnant of her old life had been snatched from her grasp.

As she passed the charred columns, tears rolled down her cheeks. Cottonwood would be hers again. She didn't know how, but it would.

❧

With supper over, Aunt Jane leaned on Savannah's arm as they made their way into the sitting room. Savannah eased her aunt down on the sofa and watched her scoot back into the cushions and settle her long skirts around her.

Savannah took in the faded dress her aunt wore and the threadbare brocade of the couch. Even if it had been six years since the end of the war, everyone she knew was still trying to recover the lifestyle they'd lost in that great conflict. Sometimes Savannah wondered if life would ever be the same again. At the moment, it didn't appear it would be for her.

Savannah settled on the floor at her aunt's feet and laid her head in the portly woman's lap. "I can't believe it," she sobbed.

"Cottonwood is gone." She'd spent most of the mealtime wiping away tears with her napkin.

Aunt Jane reached down and stroked Savannah's head. "But, darling, you knew the plantation could be bought by paying the back taxes."

Savannah straightened and stared at her aunt. "Not by somebody like him. He's not even a Southerner."

Aunt Jane frowned and picked up her fan from the table next to the sofa. "But, my dear, I thought you said he was born and raised in Mobile. The last time I checked, that was a part of the South."

Savannah waved her hand in dismissal of her aunt's words. "You know what I mean." She shivered in distaste. "I can remember how upset Poppa was when we heard that the ironworks in Selma had fallen to the Yankees and they were raiding the city. We thought they'd come to Cottonwood, but we were spared when they turned back to Montgomery. Now there's an Italian, a foreigner, living there. And on land that should belong to me."

Aunt Jane touched Savannah's lips with the still-closed fan. "You're faulting him because of his birth? Talk like that is not worthy of you. Remember, we are all God's children."

Remorse filled Savannah's heart. "I know. I suppose I'm just so shocked to think that someone stole my plantation right out from under me. I believed that God was going to answer my prayer and provide the money to pay the taxes."

Aunt Jane took hold of Savannah's arms and tugged until Savannah rose and sat on the couch next to her. "And how did you think He would do that? I hope you weren't expecting your friend Jonathan Boyer to give you that kind of money. He's only interested in making Oak Hill Plantation productive again."

Savannah blinked in surprise. "Why, Aunt Jane, you sound like you don't like Jonathan."

"I liked his mother, but I had no respect at all for his father. Any man who would treat his slaves like that man did is a disgrace to the human race. I never understood how your father could be friends with him."

"Poppa was a dreamer, Aunt Jane. He loved everybody and didn't believe anything bad about his friends."

Aunt Jane sighed, and sorrow flashed on her round face. She reached for Savannah's hand. "I know, and he let Cottonwood fall apart."

Savannah nodded. "I think the war took the heart out of him."

Aunt Jane touched a lace handkerchief to her nose and sniffed. "We all suffered during the war, maybe the Boyer family more than most. I doubt if Jonathan will ever get over being a prisoner of war at Fort Lookout Prison. That must have been an awful experience. Then to finally come home and find out his brother was killed at Gettysburg and both of his parents had died. . ." Aunt Jane paused and shook her head. "He's not the boy we knew, Savannah."

"I realize that, but you know Poppa and his father wanted us to marry and join the two farms."

"Humph! I don't put stock in folks telling you who to marry. My pa didn't want me to marry my Timothy, but I knew he was the man for me. I was right. I've watched you and Jonathan together, and I know you don't love him. At least not like I loved my Timothy."

Savannah couldn't help but smile. "I don't have too many choices around here. When you take into account how many young men died in the war and how many have left the county looking for a better life, there aren't many eligible men. There's certainly no one left who interests me. I don't think I'll ever marry."

Aunt Jane shook her head. "You don't need to unless you love someone so much that you hurt from wanting to be with him. That's the only reason to marry."

Savannah stood up. "Well, I don't ever see myself feeling like that. Maybe you and Uncle Timothy were the exceptions."

Aunt Jane rose to stand beside her. "No we weren't. There's someone like that for you. Give the good Lord time to show you."

Savannah looped her arm through her aunt's as they walked toward the hall staircase. "Well, if I ever do marry, I won't be living at Cottonwood, because it's been bought by Mr. Dante Rinaldi of Mobile."

Aunt Jane patted her hand. "The plantation may be gone, but you're still alive. And who knows what great things God has planned for you? Don't limit Him, Savannah. Let Him show you what wonderful things He has waiting for you."

Savannah leaned over and kissed her aunt on the cheek. "I don't know what I'd do without you." She glanced at the steep stairs. "Do you want me to help you upstairs to bed?"

Aunt Jane shook her head. "I can still climb my own staircase. You check things before you retire. Make sure all the lamps are out."

Savannah watched her aunt make her way to the second floor of the house and disappear into her bedroom. Walking back to the sitting room, she blew out the lamps until only one was left lit.

She picked it up and studied the flickering flame. The small light held her captive and seemed to grow into a larger blaze the longer she stared at it. A burnt smell drifted up the lamp's chimney, and she closed her eyes.

"No, I don't want to remember," Savannah moaned. "I don't

ever want to see anything like that again."

❧

Dante sat on the bluff and gazed across the rolling water of the Alabama River. With a contented sigh, he stretched out on the grassy bank, cupped his hands behind his head, and lay down. The stars twinkled brighter than he thought he'd ever seen. Maybe it just seemed so because this was a special night—his first on his own land.

He'd dreamed of this for years. At times he'd think it was in his grasp only to have it vanish like a vapor. Now it was real, and he'd never been happier. At least he told himself so.

Savannah Carmichael's anger still troubled him. It had never been his intention to let his dream destroy another's, but according to her, that's what had happened.

She'd lost so much—her parents, her home, the very existence she'd always known. In some ways, he knew how she felt. He'd lost everything, too, but a man could bury his grief in his work. For a woman, he doubted it was that easy. He hoped she would consider his offer to visit Cottonwood. That might help her some.

"Suh, you all right?"

Saul's voice from behind startled him, and he jumped to his feet. Saul held a tin lantern with a candle in it. The circle of light from it revealed the man's worried face. Dante chuckled and brushed off his pants. "I'm fine. I was just listening to the river."

Saul nodded. "It sho' can be mighty peaceable lis'nin'."

Dante stretched. "I guess it's getting late. I'd better retire if we're to get an early start tomorrow."

Saul tilted his head to one side. "What we gwine be doin'?"

Dante headed toward the house with Saul beside him. "I think we'll go into town for supplies. Tell Mamie to decide what she needs from the store, and I'll get it for her. We also need to purchase a wagon and some horses. Maybe a cow if we can find one. And tools."

Saul stopped and stared at him. "We gwine buy all that?"

Dante nodded. "There's lots to be done at Cottonwood, and the sooner we get started, the better."

Saul shook his head in wonder. "I 'spect this 'bout the bestest day of my life."

Dante smiled. "Mine, too, Saul. Mine, too."

❧

Savannah stepped inside the general store and glanced around. "Mr. Perkins?"

"Just look around. I'll be right with you." The owner's voice drifted from the room in the back.

"I'm in no hurry," she called out. *Just as long as I get out of here before Martha Thompson arrives*, she thought.

She'd come early in hopes of arriving before Martha or any of the other women in town. The news had probably already spread across Willow Bend that Cottonwood now belonged to someone else, and she couldn't bear the pitying glances she'd have to endure. Not yet, anyway.

She set the basket of eggs on the counter and waited. After a few minutes, Mr. Perkins walked from the back of the store. He smiled and wiped his hands on the long apron he wore. "Sorry, Miss Carmichael. I wanted to finish storing some of them tools that came in on the *Liberty Queen* yesterday."

The mention of the steamboat reminded her of what she'd desperately been trying to forget. She pushed the basket forward. "Aunt Jane sent me with these eggs to sell."

He peered at the contents of the basket. "Good. I need these today. I'll put them in the back."

He turned to leave, but the bell above the door jingled as

someone entered the store. "Be right with you, mister. Make yourself at home."

"Take your time."

Savannah froze at the sound of the voice. She would recognize the deep tone anywhere. Slowly she turned and stared into the smiling face of Dante Rinaldi.

"Wh—what are you doing here?"

Dante's brow wrinkled as his gaze roved over her. "The same as you, I suppose. How are you this morning, Miss Carmichael? Better than yesterday, I hope."

Her face burned, and she wanted to run from the store. She couldn't until Mr. Perkins came back. She straightened her back and clasped her hands in front of her. "I'm very well, thank you, for someone who has just been robbed of everything she had left."

If her words produced any guilt on his part, he didn't give any indication. A sad smile curled his lips. "I hope someday you'll come to see that was never my intention."

"I hardly expect that will happen."

He nodded. "Maybe not. But remember that I invited you to visit Cottonwood anytime you wish. I would never keep you from your parents' graves."

She arched an eyebrow and stared at him. "Thank you for that at least."

"Good. Then I'll expect to see you there."

At that moment, Mr. Perkins returned from the back room. "I have the amount I owe you figured up, Miss Carmichael."

She grabbed the basket from his hand. "Please apply it to our account. I'll be back with more eggs later in the week."

Without waiting for a reply, she brushed past Dante Rinaldi and hurried out the door. She stopped outside and took a deep breath. Running into the new owner of Cottonwood had been the last thing she'd expected this morning.

"Miss 'Vanna. How's you doin'?"

Her eyes widened in surprise at the sight of Saul sitting on the seat of a wagon and holding the reins of the two horses hitched to it. She took a step toward him. "Saul, where did you get this rig?"

He chuckled. "Hit ain't mine, Miss 'Vanna. Hit belongs to Mistuh Dante."

She shook her head in disbelief. "What are you doing with it?"

Saul's chest expanded with what Savannah thought must be pride. "I's workin' for Mistuh Dante now. He gwine give me money for workin' the land. Ain't that somethin'?"

Savannah's mind reeled from the second surprise of the day. How could Saul and Mamie desert her? Tears sprang to her eyes. She opened her mouth to spew out her disappointment at Saul's betrayal. Then she remembered how Saul had served her father, even when he was free, and how he'd watched over her all her life, how gently he and Mamie had tended her burns the night of the fire. She could never act spiteful to this dear man who'd been so devoted to her family. She sighed and brushed her hand across her eyes.

"I'm happy for you, Saul."

He leaned over the side of the wagon. "Cottonwood gwine be a grand place a'gin, Miss 'Vanna. Jest you wait and see. Mistuh Dante, he a good man."

Savannah's lips trembled. "I'm happy things are working out for you. Give Mamie my love."

Saul and Mamie's lives might be improving, but hers seemed to grow worse with each passing day. She clasped the straw basket tighter and hurried down the street. She had to get to Aunt Jane's house. It wouldn't do for the residents of Willow Bend to see her crying.

three

Savannah sat underneath the towering oak trees behind Aunt Jane's house and tried to concentrate on the book she held. Ever since her early morning encounters with the new owner of Cottonwood and with Saul, she'd been restless. She'd hardly touched her noon meal and had come outside to get some air after Aunt Jane lay down for an afternoon nap.

With a start, she realized she had not turned a page in at least ten minutes. Her thoughts kept returning to Dante Rinaldi. Every reasonable thought told her she should hate the handsome Italian, but for some reason, she couldn't. Maybe it was how he had returned her anger with kindness. It had been gracious of him to invite her to visit her parents' graves.

She sighed and raised the book. Perhaps she'd go tomorrow or the next day.

A horse galloped to a stop in front of the house, and a voice rang out. "Savannah, where are you?"

She smiled at the sound of Jonathan Boyer's voice. "In the backyard."

Jonathan ran around the corner of the house and strode toward her. He held his hat in his hand and pointed at her with it as he walked. His brows were drawn into a fierce frown. "I came as soon as I heard."

Savannah rose from the chair and laid her book in it. "Jonathan, what's the matter?"

Anger shone in his blue eyes, and he raked his hand through

his brown hair. "Cottonwood has been sold?"

"Yes," she said. "How did you find out?"

"I heard it at the general store. Mr. Perkins said the new owner came in and bought supplies this morning."

She reached out and placed her hand on his arm. "He did. I was there when he arrived."

He stepped back, his eyes wide. "You've seen him?"

She nodded. "Yes. I met him yesterday."

His eyes narrowed. "What's he like?"

Savannah hesitated before she replied. If she was honest, she would say she sensed kindness in him. He'd seemed truly sorry at her distress, and he'd given Saul and Mamie what her family hadn't been able to do since the war. Still, he was her enemy, and she needed to remember that.

"He's Italian," she finally said.

He stepped back in surprise. "An Italian? I should have known that no Southerner would have stolen your land."

Savannah remembered her conversation with Aunt Jane. "He's from Mobile."

Jonathan's eyes narrowed. "Mr. Perkins said he looked like he was in his early thirties. Mr. Perkins asked him if he fought in the war, and he said he hadn't. Can you believe that? He's not only an Italian, but he let men like me rot in a prison camp and my brother die in battle instead of helping our cause."

The anger in Jonathan's face deepened. It seemed everything that upset Jonathan always related back to the war in some way. Savannah sighed. "We've got to quit fighting the war, Jonathan. It's been over for six years."

Jonathan recoiled from her as if she'd slapped him. "How can you say that after all we've lost? Cottonwood is just one more tragedy of the war's aftermath, and now it's in the hands of an Italian."

Tears flooded her eyes. "Whatever the reason, it's gone."

Jonathan propped his hands on his hips and shook his head. "I can't believe it. How did he get it?"

She wiped her eyes and shrugged. "Paid the taxes."

She sat back down and motioned for him to take the other chair, but he shook his head. He began to pace up and down in front of her. "Cottonwood was supposed to be mine."

"Yours?" Startled, Savannah grabbed the arms of the chair and stared at him.

Jonathan dropped to one knee beside her and covered her hand with his. "I meant ours. Isn't that what our families wanted?"

"B–b–but that was just talk between our parents. You and I have never been more than friends."

He reached up and cupped her chin with his hand. "Forgive me, Savannah. I didn't mean to upset you." He stood up and stared down at her. "Don't worry about this. Let me take care of it."

The determined look on Jonathan's face scared Savannah. She jumped up. "What are you going to do?"

He smiled, grasped her hand again, and raised it to his mouth. His lips felt warm to her skin, and pleasure flowed through her. He straightened and let go of her. "I'll do whatever's necessary to get that land back."

Without another word, he turned and rushed across the yard. Within moments she heard the sound of his horse galloping down the road. Jonathan's visit troubled her. He'd never acted possessive or given her orders before. Why would he do it now? Perhaps the loss of the land disturbed him more than it did her.

His words and the tone of his voice troubled her. Maybe a visit to her parents' graves would settle her down. She picked up her book and headed for the house. She'd get Jasper to hitch the horse to the buggy, and then she'd go to Cottonwood.

Savannah stopped before she entered the back door. What would she do if she encountered Dante Rinaldi again? No need to worry about that. He'd probably be working away from the river, and he'd never know she'd been there.

⋅⋙⋅

Dante stooped down, scooped up a handful of soil, and raised it to his nose. The smell of the earth always excited him, but this was something different. This was his land, and it held promise for the future. He spread his fingers and let the dirt sift through them.

"This ground is going to grow some good corn."

Saul pulled off his hat and wiped at the sweat on his forehead. "Yas suh. If'n we evah git this here canebrake cleaned out. We shoulda brought Abraham and Joshua 'stead of leavin' them to clear off the front of where the big house sat."

Dante rose and glanced across the area where they'd worked all afternoon. When he'd first seen the dense growth of the field, he thought it would take no time for Saul and him to clear it. Now he realized how wrong he'd been. Even with the help of Abraham and Joshua, Saul's sons, it would take longer than he'd thought.

The majestic cane stalks with their daggerlike green leaves towered above their heads. He estimated their height anywhere from fifteen to thirty feet, and they grew closely together, forming an almost impenetrable barrier. Even the birds that flew among the branches of the trees along the edge of the canebrake didn't enter the dense vegetation.

"I think you have a point, Saul. We need some help." He thought for a moment before he spoke again. "Do you know any other men who'd like to come to Cottonwood as tenants?"

Saul's mouth pulled into another of his huge grins. "You means like me and Mamie? Workin' on the shares?"

Dante nodded. "That's right. All I can offer them right now is a place to live in the old quarters. But we've got to get some of this land cleared by spring." He glanced down at the rich soil. "I've never seen anything like this fertile earth. We could grow enough corn on it to feed an army."

"I knows lotsa men a-wantin' to work."

"Then we'll start visiting them tomorrow." Dante laughed and slapped Saul on the shoulder. "There's no time to waste."

Saul let out a whoop. "Yas suh, we gwine grow us some corn."

Dante chuckled at the excitement on the man's face. "And lots of cotton, too. But I think we've done about all the good we can here until we get some help. What say we go see what Mamie's cooked us for supper?"

Saul glanced up at the sky and bent to pick up the ax he'd been using. "I s'pose hit 'bout quittin' time."

Together they loaded the tools in the wagon at the edge of the field. They climbed aboard, and Saul guided the horse through the dense growth toward the bluff. Within minutes Dante spied the rolling water through the trees.

As the wagon drove along the bluff, Dante stared across the wide expanse of water and wondered how far it was to the opposite bank. Perhaps someday he'd try rowing across to the other side, but that would have to wait. Right now he had more pressing matters—like clearing additional land.

He'd been disappointed when he first saw the amount of tillable soil left at the plantation. Evidently with no slave labor available after the war, Vance Carmichael had let most of the fields return to their natural state. If Dante was going to bring in more tenant farmers, he would need extra acreage for planting.

The thought of Vance Carmichael brought to mind his daughter. Every time Dante thought of her, his heart stirred. Her anguish at losing the plantation had caused him to lie awake last night. Or maybe it was more than her distress. It could be that he found her to be a fascinating young woman. As much as he tried to fight it, she'd occupied his thoughts ever since he'd stared up at her when she almost ran him down.

With a sigh, he straightened on the wagon seat as they rounded the path leading back to the front of the old mansion. The fence of the cemetery came into sight, and his heart pounded in his chest. Her buggy stood outside the fence.

Saul pulled the horse to a stop. "Miss 'Vanna's heah."

Dante swallowed and looked around, but he didn't see her anywhere. Then he spied her sitting underneath one of the water oaks beside her parents' graves. She leaned against the trunk of the tree, her eyes closed.

Dante climbed down. "I'll check on her."

He walked through the gate and stopped in front of her. His chest contracted and squeezed his pounding heart as he stared down at her. He'd never been affected by any woman the way she stirred him, and it frightened him.

Love had been something he thought he'd never find, and the last thing he needed was to have feelings for a woman who hated him. As he gazed at her, he knew he was helpless to ignore it. No matter what she thought of him, she had cast a spell on him.

She stirred in her sleep, and he backed away.

ॐ

Savannah dug her knuckles into her eyes in an effort to wake. She hadn't meant to drift off; but the day had been so nice, and it was so peaceful here. Her eyes fluttered open, and she shrank against the tree trunk. A man stood over her.

Fear rose in her as her gaze traveled up the man's body and came to rest on Dante Rinaldi's face. He leaned over her, a worried expression on his face. "Are you all right, Miss Carmichael?"

She scrambled to her feet. "I'm fine."

In an effort to push past him, she took a step but caught the hem of her dress under her foot. Arms flailing, she pitched toward him.

His strong hands grasped her shoulders and steadied her before he released her. He backed away. "I didn't mean to frighten you. I saw you under the tree and thought you might be ill."

Her shoulders burned from the contact with him. Had his touch blistered her skin? Her bonnet lay on the ground next to the tree, and she bent to retrieve it. "I—I sat down for a minute, and I suppose I fell asleep."

The corners of his eyes crinkled. "Then I'm glad I came along. You might have spent the entire night on the ground."

Samantha glanced across the river, and panic overcame her at the sun sinking into the west. "Oh, I didn't realize it was so late. Aunt Jane will be worried." She stepped around him and headed for her buggy. "I need to go."

He followed and closed the gate to the cemetery. Saul, who'd climbed down from the wagon, held the reins of her horse. "Afte'noon, Miss 'Vanna. It sho' is good to see you ag'in."

She smiled. "It's good to see you, too."

Saul pointed over his shoulder. "Me and Mistuh Dante been a-cleanin' out that ole canebrake. Reckon we gwine grow some mighty good corn there."

Savannah raised her eyebrows and turned back to Dante, who'd stopped beside the buggy. "Clearing the canebrakes?

That's a big job for two men. I doubt if you'll be able to accomplish it."

He nodded. "I think you're right. That's why I told Saul we needed more tenant farmers."

She narrowed her gaze and studied the self-assured man. "If you want more tenants, you might check out at the Crossroads. There's a shantytown filled with men who need work." She nodded toward Saul. "Saul knows the way."

Dante's eyes sparkled. "Thank you, Miss Carmichael. It's kind of you to tell me."

She could hardly believe she'd given him that information, but anybody in Willow Bend could have told him. Perhaps some of Cottonwood's former slaves who lived there would be able to return.

It was hard to ignore the thrill that she'd felt at the news they were clearing more land. After the slaves had been freed, she'd begged her father to bring in tenant farmers as many of the other planters were doing. He'd refused, and the land had suffered. It seemed the new owner intended to restore the land to what it had once been.

As if Saul could read her thoughts, he spoke. "Big Mike and Pinky live out to the Crossroads. Maybe they's can come back home."

His words pierced her heart. The former slaves might return, but she knew she never would. She fought back tears and climbed into the buggy. Dante took the reins from Saul and handed them to her.

"It's getting late, Miss Carmichael. I'd be happy to follow you home."

In his face she saw genuine concern for her safety, but she couldn't be swayed by his attempts to gain her friendship. He was still her enemy. She turned a cool look toward him.

"Home? Haven't you heard? I don't have one anymore."

She snapped the reins, and the horse surged forward.

❧

Saul, a confused expression on his face, turned to Dante. "What she mean she ain't got no home?"

Dante shook his head. "Miss Carmichael's angry at me for buying her land."

Saul's mouth formed a large circle. "Oh."

They walked back to the wagon and climbed aboard. Neither spoke all the way back to the cabins. The sting of Savannah's words echoed through Dante's mind. There had to be some way he could make her understand his position. He'd worked and saved for years, and now he couldn't abandon his dream. Not even for a woman who filled his thoughts and made him long for something that could never be.

The wagon rumbled to a stop outside the still-standing barn. Dante was thankful that Saul and his sons had kept it in good repair.

"Go on, Mistuh Dante. I'll take care of the hosses."

Dante hopped from the wagon and nodded. "Thanks."

He strode toward the cabin where he was living. It sat away from the rows of ramshackle buildings where slaves had once lived, but it wasn't much better than the other houses. He stopped on the front porch and clutched one of the posts that supported the extended roof.

When the additional tenant farmers came, perhaps building new cabins should be one of the priorities. Men worked better when they had adequate housing and food. He'd wanted to have a good portion of the land producing by next spring, but perhaps he needed a new timeline. He had to provide for his workers first.

He stepped through the door and glanced around at the

dreary interior of the two-room cabin. And what about himself? He also needed better quarters. What if he decided to marry? A woman would have to love a man a lot to share such a life as his.

Certainly a woman like Savannah Carmichael would want better. She'd been used to the best, not a cabin built of rotting wood.

He raked his hand through his hair and groaned. "Why can't I quit thinking about her?"

Walking back to the front door, he looked out across the hard-packed earth that covered the area where the cabins stood. Mamie would bring him some supper in a while, but she'd go back to Saul and her sons. He'd be alone like so many other nights in the past, but tonight the loneliness crushed him more than ever.

The vision of Savannah Carmichael drifted through his thoughts, and the words she'd spoken sent guilt racing through his body.

"Home? Haven't you heard? I don't have one anymore."

four

Dante strode from the cabin as soon as the sun was up the next morning. He ignored the ache in his back and shoulders from the labor in the canebrake the day before. The pain was little enough to bear if it meant his land would be cleared and ready for planting by spring.

Today he and Saul were going to the Crossroads to see if they could enlist more men to join them as tenant farmers. From what Saul had told him, the freed slaves couldn't wait to get away from Cottonwood, but they had found it hard to live on their own. Maybe some of them would want to come back to the land they'd worked for the Carmichaels. This time, though, they would be working for themselves.

"Good mornin', Mistuh Dante."

The voice startled him, and he turned as Saul rounded the corner of the cabin. "I didn't see you there. What are you doing out so early?"

Saul's eyes grew wide. "The sun done come up, so it's time to git to work. Mamie got you some breakfast cooked. Come on over and eat."

Dante smiled. "I hope she's made some more biscuits like those she had last night."

Saul laughed and slapped his leg. "I ain't never seen no woman so happy to have anything as she was what you done bought yestiday. It's been a long time since we had such good eatin'. I 'spect the Lord blessed us when you come to Cottonwood."

Savannah Carmichael's face flashed before his eyes, but he

tried to ignore her words that still rang through his mind. "I hope I can be a blessing to more than just your family, Saul. If we can get some more tenant farmers and get the fields ready for planting, we can restore Miss Carmichael's land to what it was before the war."

Saul pulled off the straw hat he wore, held it in front of him, and gazed down at the ground. "I don't means to be speakin' bad about Mistuh Vance, but the land done started to grow wild 'fore the war came. He never seemed to know what to do like his pappy did. Now Miss 'Vanna, she got a good head on her shoulders. After the war, she tried to talk to Mistuh Vance 'bout gittin' some tenant farmers to help clear those canebrakes and plantin' more crops, but he wouldn't listen. Sometimes I thought even if Miss 'Vanna was just a young girl, she ought to be runnin' Cottonwood."

Dante smiled and glanced up at the sun. "We better hurry. After we eat, I want to leave right away for the Crossroads. We've got a big day ahead of us, Saul."

Saul nodded. "I 'spect we do, Mr. Dante. I 'spect we do."

❧

Two hours later, Dante stood in the center of the shantytown known as the Crossroads. The makeshift hovels that dotted the area made the abandoned slave quarters at Cottonwood look like comfortable houses. Saul had told him he didn't know how many people lived in the small community that had sprung up after the war, and he couldn't estimate the number either.

Small children ran along the dirt paths that twisted between the shelters, and a group of older young people sat underneath a tree to his left. Suspicion gleamed in their unblinking eyes. He wondered what memories had made them wary of strangers. He smiled, but they gave no response.

The horses harnessed to the wagon snorted and swished their tails as the August sun climbed higher in the morning sky. Dante patted the one he stood beside and stared down the path where Saul had disappeared ten minutes ago. Perhaps he was having trouble persuading any of the men to come to talk to the stranger from Mobile.

When Dante thought he could bear the stares of the young people no longer, Saul appeared at the end of the path. Four men walked behind him. Dante's eyes grew wide at the sight of a young white man in the group. The others had skin the color of Saul's, and they walked forward with their gazes directed at Dante.

As they approached, Saul broke into a grin that radiated confidence. The group stopped in front of Dante, and he let his gaze drift over their faces.

Saul pointed to a tall, muscular man dressed in overalls and a long-sleeved shirt. "This here Big Mike. He was over the field hands at Cottonwood, and he knows that land better'n anybody in these here parts."

Dante stuck out his hand. "It's good to meet you, Big Mike. I'm Dante Rinaldi."

Big Mike glanced down at the outstretched hand and hesitated before he reached out and grasped it. "Suh," he said.

Saul pointed to the others behind him. "And this here's Pinky. I tole you 'bout him. He kin pick mo' cotton in a day than anybody I ever seen."

Dante pumped Pinky's hand. "Sounds like you're what we need at Cottonwood."

Pinky grinned and shifted from foot to foot. "I sho' would like to pick in them fields agin."

Sweat glimmered on the dark brow of the man standing next to Pinky. He glanced at Dante's hand but didn't pull his from his pockets. "My name Mose. Mr. Boyer owned me 'fore the war, and I worked his place."

Dante let his hand drift to his side and stared Mose in the eye. "Nobody owns you now, Mose."

The man took a deep breath. "Naw suh, I 'spect they don't."

Dante looked past Saul at the white man, who appeared to be barely old enough to shave. "And what's your name?"

The boy grinned, and Dante noticed two bottom teeth missing. "I'm Henry Walton. Grew up in Georgia. After the war, there weren't nothing left for me there. Folks all dead. So me and my wife started west. Thought we might end up in Texas. We got this far and found these good folks and decided to stay for the winter."

"Are you planning on moving on in the spring?"

Henry shrugged. "Depends on what I find here."

Dante smiled and glanced around at the faces of the men. "I suppose Saul has told you that I need some workers to help me farm my new land. Right now I can't offer you much. I'm staying in one of the slave quarters myself, as are Saul and his family. You'll have to do the same. But we'll build you houses so you can have a little spot that's yours, and I'll let you farm a portion of the land on shares. I'll see that you get some livestock to start off, but it'll be up to you to take care of it. If you prosper, it'll be because of your efforts, not mine. I've worked hard to get this land. I'll expect you to do the same, or I'll find someone to take your place. What do you say?"

Henry Walton nodded. "Best offer I've had since I left Georgia. I reckon as how me and my wife gonna take you up on it, Mr. Rinaldi."

"Good." Dante glanced at the other men. "Anybody else?"

Big Mike looked at Mose and Pinky then back to Dante. "Saul says we can trust you. So I 'spect we be going to

Cottonwood if you let us bring our families."

Dante laughed. "Of course. I suppose I thought that was understood. I'm not married, but I want there to be families on the land. I want to hear children running and laughing. I want to bring life back to a grand plantation."

Saul smacked his hands together and giggled. "I guess that what we gwine do, Mistuh Dante. We gwine bring life back to a dead place."

"When do you want to move?" Dante asked.

Big Mike's eyebrows arched. "We be ready in a few minutes."

Dante frowned. "Do we have enough room on my wagon to transport all your belongings?"

"I got a small wagon," Henry said. "Between yours and mine, I think we got enough room."

Dante glanced at his wagon. It wasn't very big. "How many women and children will there be?"

Henry thought for a moment. "We've all got wives, and each family has three children except for Mary Ann and me. We ain't got one yet."

Dante shook his head. "We only have two wagons to transport your belongings and, counting Saul and me, nineteen people. Maybe I need to get some extra help."

Big Mike smiled at Dante. "No need for that. We kin walk."

"But it's at least ten miles from here to Cottonwood."

"That don't matter."

Dante chuckled. "Then we'll all take turns walking. Now go get your belongings, and let's head out."

The men stood still a moment as if they couldn't believe what had happened, and then with a whoop, they ran back the way they'd come. Twenty minutes later, Dante and Saul stood beside the two wagons and surveyed the small number of personal objects the families had placed there. Henry's small wagon was almost filled, but Dante's still had room.

Dante turned to the assembled group. The women stood almost hidden behind their husbands, with their children at their sides. The woman standing next to Mose held a small infant in her arms. Dante wondered how long it had been since she'd given birth.

He turned to Saul and whispered in his ear. "Is that Mose's wife with the baby?"

"Yas suh."

Dante cleared his throat and faced the group again. "We have room for some of the women and younger children to ride in my wagon." He nodded to Mose. "Mose, help your wife into the wagon."

The woman hugged her baby tighter, but Mose shook his head. "Tildy can walk. She strong."

Dante sighed and glanced at Saul, who shrugged. He turned back to the group. "I appreciate the fact that your wife doesn't want any preferential treatment, but she's weak. I won't have it on my conscience that I let a woman who's recently given birth walk all the way back to Cottonwood. Now it's your choice. She rides in the wagon, or you unpack your belongings and stay here."

Mose started to object, but he looked down at his wife. His shoulders sagged, and he faced Dante. "Much obliged, Mistuh Dante. I reckon ain't no white man ever wanted to help one of mine before."

Dante stepped forward. "Things have changed, Mose. It's a new day in the South."

Mose's eyes narrowed. "I reckon for some, but not all."

Dante glanced at Saul, who nodded. "Folks at the Boyer plantation weren't never treated like Mistuh Vance did us what lived at Cottonwood. Oak Hill be a hard place to live as a slave."

Before Dante could question him, Saul stepped forward and picked up a small girl who appeared to be about three years old. Mose lifted his wife and baby into the wagon, and Saul set the child he held next to her.

Dante smiled and glanced at the children still standing beside the wagon. "Now you fathers decide who's going to walk and who's going to ride on the first leg of the journey."

When the wagon was filled, Dante turned to Big Mike. "Saul and I will walk the first leg, and then we'll take turns with the wagon. Do you want to lead the way?"

Big Mike's eyes grew wide. "Suh, you wants me to handle the hosses?"

Dante nodded. "I expect you know how from your years at Cottonwood."

A smile broke out on Big Mike's face, and he climbed into the wagon seat. Wrapping the reins around his hands, he released the brake and cracked the reins across the horses' backs. "Giddap, you hosses. We's goin' home."

Home. The word warmed Dante's heart and stirred him in a way he'd never known. His father's dream had been to own some of Alabama's rich, black farmland, but yellow fever had ended that desire. Now it was Dante's turn to fulfill the hope his parents had when they settled in Mobile.

Dante watched the wagons rumble by, leading the way. He stepped aside as those walking behind passed him. Some of the women, their skin glistening in the hot sun and their hair covered by tattered bonnets, darted a glance his way, but most of them directed their attention straight ahead.

There was no laughter from the children, and this surprised Dante. He was overcome by the realization that he had no idea what these people had experienced in their lives. Now another white man had come with his promises. Perhaps they were too afraid to trust him yet. But they would.

With God's help, he would teach them to trust. And the land was going to help him do that.

five

Two weeks after Savannah heard that tenant farmers had come to Cottonwood, she sat in the church where she had worshipped all her life. The pastor had been preaching for fifteen minutes, but this morning she didn't hear his words.

She glanced at the few worshippers who'd gathered. When she was growing up, the church had been filled on Sundays. Buggies and wagons loaded with families streamed into the churchyard. Sundays were reserved for worship and, afterward, for visiting with friends and neighbors. Planters discussed their crops, women shared secrets, and children chased each other across the lawn.

Sunday worship, as well as everything else in her life, changed when the first young men left to join the Confederate forces. Too many familiar faces were with them no longer.

Even six years after the end of the war, its effects haunted each family she knew. She caught a glimpse of the Redmans from the plantation closest to Cottonwood. With both of their sons killed in the conflict, they had long ago moved to Willow Bend and left their land to be sold for back taxes just as hers had been.

Resentment rose up in her throat, and she tried to swallow the choking rage at the thought of Dante Rinaldi living on her land. It had been more than two weeks since she'd seen the man but not since she'd heard about him.

Every time she went to the store to sell their eggs, she ran into Martha Thompson, who couldn't wait to tell her what

44

she'd heard was going on at Cottonwood. The new owner had brought in four families to work as tenant farmers, she had said. One of them was white. At this statement, Martha's eyebrows arched, and her nostrils flared.

"Can you imagine white people living out there in that shantytown?" she said. "All I can say is that they must be white trash."

Savannah had turned away and tried to focus on selling her eggs, but the news hadn't been unexpected. After all, she had encouraged Mr. Rinaldi to go to the Crossroads. Although she would never admit it, she was pleased that the land would be worked again. If only her father had listened to her, she might be the one getting ready for next spring at Cottonwood. Instead, an Italian, with dark eyes that made her breath catch in her throat, would harvest the next crop on her land.

Turning her head slightly, she glanced over her shoulder, and her heart thudded. Dante Rinaldi sat in the last pew. His dark stare bored into her, and he nodded in her direction. For a moment, she froze before she blinked and jerked her head around.

Aunt Jane, who sat on her right, frowned and leaned toward her. "What's the matter?"

Savannah bit her lip and shook her head. She patted her aunt's hand. "Nothing."

Smiling, Savannah straightened her shoulders and directed her attention back to the pastor. Aunt Jane continued to look at her, but after a moment, she unfolded the fan that lay in her lap and began to wave it back and forth in the lazy fashion Savannah had seen her do so many times.

For the remainder of the sermon, thoughts of the man who sat in the rear of the church whirled through her head. What would she say to him? After all, she had invited him to church, but that was before she knew he was her enemy. Even if she didn't like him, she reasoned, she couldn't be rude in a house of worship.

When "Amen" was uttered, she turned to Aunt Jane and stole a quick glance toward the back pew. Her heart plummeted at the sight of the empty bench. She scanned the congregation, but he was nowhere to be seen.

A wave of disappointment washed over her. Why should she care if he left? She should be thankful she'd been saved another embarrassing meeting with him.

As the few church members walked up the aisle, everyone stopped to speak to Aunt Jane before they moved on to Reverend Somers, who stood at the entrance.

When the last one walked by, Aunt Jane stepped into the aisle. "How many were here today?"

"I counted twenty." Savannah shook her head. "No, twenty-one. I forgot the visitor."

Aunt Jane's eyebrows arched. "I didn't see a new face. Who was it?"

Savannah took her aunt by the arm and nudged her up the aisle. "Dante Rinaldi sat in the back, but he's already gone."

Aunt Jane stopped and gazed at Savannah. "I wish I could have met him. Maybe another time."

"Maybe."

Reverend Somers smiled as they approached. "Mrs. Martin, it's so good to see you again." He nodded to Savannah. "And you, too, Miss Carmichael."

Aunt Jane closed her fan and stuck it in her reticule. "Very good sermon, Reverend. I understand we had a visitor."

"Yes, but he left before I could greet him. Maybe he'll come again. Do you know him?"

"Savannah tells me he's the new owner of Cottonwood."

Reverend Somers gave a small gasp. "I had no idea." He cleared his throat. "I need to get something from the front of the church, but if you'll wait, I'll be glad to help you down the steps."

Aunt Jane waved her hand in protest. "No need for that. Savannah and I can make it fine. Have a nice day, Reverend."

"And you, too."

As the pastor walked away, Aunt Jane took a deep breath and grasped Savannah's arm. "Come, Savannah. Let's go."

Aunt Jane's weight sagged against Savannah, and a sense of alarm rose in her. "Do you feel all right?"

"Yes. I'm just a little short of breath. Nothing to be concerned about."

Savannah led her aunt out of the church and stopped to catch a better hold of her arm at the front steps.

"Allow me to assist you, Miss Carmichael."

Savannah straightened and stared into the face of Dante Rinaldi, who stood at the foot of the steps. Her heart pounded, and a slow breath trickled from her mouth. "Thank you, Mr. Rinaldi."

He positioned himself on the other side of Aunt Jane. Together they eased her down the steps. When they stopped at the bottom, Aunt Jane took a deep breath and turned to Dante. "You must be the new owner of Cottonwood. Savannah has told me about you."

A smile curled his lips. "I hope she didn't convince you I'm some sort of ogre."

Aunt Jane chuckled. "Not at all, Mr. Rinaldi. In fact, I've found myself wondering about you. You should call on us sometime so we can get better acquainted."

"I'd like that."

Savannah glanced around at the people who'd already climbed

into their buggies. Never had she seen such looks of loathing, and they were directed at Dante. She recognized the silent message her friends were sending. Interlopers who bought land for back taxes weren't welcome in their closed Southern society.

Guilt flowed through her, and her skin burned. Was she responsible for the community's opinion of Dante? She considered the misfortune of losing her land a problem for her, not a cause that her friends should embrace. She tightened her grip on her aunt's arm. "I'm sure Mr. Rinaldi has better things to do than to stand around talking to two women, and you're tired. Let's get you home."

Dante appeared oblivious to her neighbors' glares. "I believe I see your buggy tied to that tree. I'll walk you there."

Savannah opened her mouth to protest, but Dante was already propelling her aunt across the yard. With a sigh, she followed behind.

When they reached the buggy, Aunt Jane turned to Dante. "How do you like living at Cottonwood, Mr. Rinaldi?"

"I find myself enjoying it, even though we're working very hard."

Savannah watched the last buggy pull from the churchyard before she glanced at Dante. "I hear you have more tenant farmers now. How is that working out?"

"Fine. They're all very hard workers. We're going to try and build some better housing for them before winter, but getting the land ready for spring planting is the main goal right now."

Savannah nodded. "I can understand that."

His gaze flitted across her face. "I haven't seen you at your parents' graves lately."

Her skin warmed more under his intense stare. "I come when you're in the fields. I don't want to be in anybody's way."

His eyes clouded. "It's always a pleasure to have you there."

"Thank you." She turned back to her aunt. "Now, let's get—" She stopped in horror at the grimace on her aunt's face. "Aunt Jane, what's the matter?"

She clutched at her chest. "I'm not feeling well."

Before Savannah could react, Aunt Jane's eyes widened, and she slumped toward the ground. In one swift motion, Dante caught her in his arms.

Fear washed over Savannah. "Aunt Jane, what's happening?"

Her aunt's eyelids drooped, and she struggled to breathe. "My heart."

Dante lifted her into the seat of the buggy and helped Savannah climb in beside her.

"Take your aunt home. I'll get the doctor. I know where his office is."

Aunt Jane tried to straighten in the seat. "May not be there. Wasn't in church today."

Dante gave Aunt Jane's hand a squeeze. "Don't worry. I'll find him no matter where he is and follow him to your house."

Dante ran to the tree and untied the reins. As he handed them to her, Savannah couldn't hide the trembling in her hands. "Thank you."

Dante looped the reins around her fingers and covered her shaking hands with his. "Don't worry. I'll be there with the doctor."

Savannah bit her lip and flicked the reins across the horse's back. As the buggy sped from the churchyard, Dante's horse galloped past in a cloud of dust. She couldn't take her eyes off the straight back and broad shoulders of the man riding ahead. He hunched forward as he spurred the horse on, and she clenched the reins tighter.

Her lips thinned into a straight line at the thought of their friends and neighbors leaving them at the church. Some of them must have noticed Aunt Jane's labored steps and her collapse. If Dante hadn't been there, she didn't know what she would have done.

She might tell herself that Dante Rinaldi was her enemy, but in her heart, she knew better. From their first meeting, she had known this man was different from any she'd met before. Now he rode to get help for them. A thought that she could never voice popped into her head. She was glad he was the one who'd come to their aid.

❧

An hour later, Savannah sat on the sofa in the parlor where she often sat with Aunt Jane. Dante stood at the window and stared outside. He had done as he said. She and Jasper had just gotten Aunt Jane out of the buggy and into the house when Dante arrived with the doctor.

Again Dante had scooped Aunt Jane up and carried her up the stairs as if she were weightless. Jasper shuffled behind, insisting with each breath that he was still able to take care of his friend.

Savannah stood, walked to the foot of the steps, and stared up to the second floor. Jasper paced back and forth in the hallway. Sighing, Savannah headed back to the parlor.

"What could be taking Dr. Spencer so long?"

Dante turned toward her. "I'm sure he'll let us know something soon."

The sound of hoofbeats outside caught her attention. "Who is that?"

Dante pulled the curtain back and looked outside. "A man just rode up. He's coming into the house."

The front door burst open, and Jonathan Boyer strode into the parlor. He crossed the floor and grabbed Savannah's hands. "I came as soon as I heard about your aunt. How is she?"

"The doctor's still with her. Maybe we'll know something soon."

Jonathan started to say something else but stopped when he spied Dante. A frown wrinkled his brow. He stared first at Dante then back at Savannah. "I'm sorry. I didn't know you had company." Turning to Dante, he took a step toward him. "I don't think we've met. I'm Jonathan Boyer, the owner of Oak Hill Plantation. I'm a friend of Savannah's."

Dante stuck out his hand. "I'm Dante Rinaldi."

A red flush started at the base of Jonathan's neck and spread upward. "I've heard of you. You're the thief who stole Cottonwood?"

Dante's hand drifted back to his side. "Bought it, not stole it."

Savannah touched Jonathan's arm. "Mr. Rinaldi helped me with Aunt Jane today. It was fortunate for me that he was at church."

"Quite right, Miss Carmichael." Dr. Spencer stood in the doorway. A deep frown furrowed his brow.

Savannah hurried toward him. "How is my aunt? Is it her heart again?"

He set his medical bag down and reached for Savannah's hand. "Yes, but she's resting now. I'm afraid I've done everything I can. Her body is worn out. I think you have to prepare yourself for the inevitable."

The sympathy she heard in his voice reminded her how he'd talked with her after her parents' deaths. A tear trickled from Savannah's eye, but she bit her lip and nodded. "I know. It's just that I can't imagine life without her."

"And she's concerned about you, too. I can't tell you how long she has. So put it in God's hands and enjoy each day."

Savannah nodded. "I will."

Dr. Spencer released her hand. "It was a pleasure to meet

you, Mr. Rinaldi. I hope to see you again soon."

Dante crossed the room to shake the doctor's hand. "Thank you, Dr. Spencer. I wish we could have met under better circumstances. Maybe the next time we see each other, no one will be ill."

The doctor chuckled. "I hope so." He nodded to Jonathan, turned, and walked toward the door.

When the door closed behind Dr. Spencer, Savannah faced Dante. "Thank you again, Mr. Rinaldi, for your help. I know you must have other things to do this afternoon, so don't let me keep you."

His eyes widened with surprise, and Savannah felt a moment of guilt. He must think her ungracious to dismiss him so abruptly, but she feared his presence was upsetting Jonathan.

She smiled and led the way to the front door. Dante followed.

When she opened it, he stood in front of her for a moment. "If you need me for anything, Miss Carmichael, please let me know."

She extended her hand. "I will. And thank you again. I don't know what I would have done if you hadn't been there."

He looked down at her hand before he clasped it in his. For a brief moment, he squeezed her fingers then released them and strode from the house. He mounted his horse and rode away without looking back.

Savannah stepped onto the porch and watched until he disappeared. The day had produced some strange reactions in her. During the worship service, she had fumed because her enemy had come to her church. Afterward she discovered that a kind soul inhabited the body of the man she wanted to hate.

Now a new realization spread through her: Dante Rinaldi wasn't her enemy. What he was, she didn't yet know, but she looked forward to finding out.

six

Savannah stared at the coffin being lowered into the ground. She wondered why there were no tears on her face. Perhaps she had shed them all in the month since Aunt Jane's attack at church. Or it could be that her body was too exhausted from the constant care her aunt had needed in the past weeks.

Whatever the reason, Savannah felt empty inside. The last link to the life she'd known had now disappeared. Her parents, Cottonwood and its inhabitants, and now Aunt Jane were gone. She had nothing left.

Beside her, Jasper wiped at the tears streaming down his face. He had been diligent in his attention to Aunt Jane in her last days, just as he had been all his life. It dawned on her that they shared something in common now—neither of them had anyone or anything left.

She glanced around at the mourners gathered in the cemetery. All the town's residents had turned out for the funeral of one of Willow Bend's most loved women. Her gaze drifted across the people she'd known all her life and came to rest on a lone figure standing behind the group.

Dante Rinaldi nodded a silent greeting. His eyes held her hostage for a moment before she glanced away.

Jonathan stood across the grave from her. He frowned and looked from her to Dante before he directed his attention back to Reverend Somers. Savannah sighed and did the same.

With the graveside service completed, Jonathan stood beside her as she greeted every person there. From time to time, she searched the crowd for Dante, but he had disappeared.

After shaking hands with the last mourner, Jonathan turned to her. "I'll take you home."

She shook her head. "There's no need. Jasper can drive us. You probably need to get back home."

"I always have time for you, Savannah. I thought you knew that."

Savannah inwardly flinched at the words. Since the day he'd encountered Dante in her parlor, Jonathan had returned only once to check on their welfare. Dante, on the other hand, had stopped by at least once a week. She'd found herself looking forward to his visits. It surprised her to find out that he was nothing like she first thought. In fact, she had come to like him.

In the last days of Aunt Jane's life, she often talked about Dante's kind nature, and Savannah realized her aunt had been right. She pushed her thoughts from her mind and smiled at Jonathan. "To tell you the truth, I think Jasper and I need to be alone. These last few weeks have been difficult, and I just want to rest for a while."

Jonathan nodded. "I understand. If you need me for anything, send Jasper to Oak Hill to get me."

"I will. Thank you for coming today."

Jonathan walked to his horse at the edge of the cemetery and climbed into the saddle. With a wave, he galloped away.

Savannah turned to Jasper, who hadn't said a word since they'd left home. "Are you ready to go, Jasper?"

He nodded and trudged behind her toward the buggy. His footsteps rustled in the leaves that had begun to fall from the oak trees rimming the cemetery. Savannah took a deep breath and smiled. Fall would soon arrive, and nature would paint its landscape with all the brilliant colors she loved.

She always looked forward to fall because nature changed

so drastically to welcome the cold days ahead. Now she needed to adjust her life to get ready for all the challenges that lay ahead. Everything she'd known was gone, and uncertainty loomed before her.

When they reached the buggy, Jasper helped her climb in and then walked to the tree where he'd tied the horse. His stiff fingers fumbled with the reins. With a sinking heart, Savannah realized Jasper was getting old, too.

As he turned to get in beside her, a flash of color emerged from the tree line at the back of the cemetery. Dante, sitting straight on his black horse, rode toward her. She pressed her hand to her chest to still her thumping heart.

Dante pulled the horse to a stop next to the buggy and removed his hat. "I wanted to offer my condolences."

She clasped her hands in her lap so he wouldn't see how they shook. "Thank you, Mr. Rinaldi. It was kind of you to come. I saw you at the grave site, but I thought you'd left."

His eyes narrowed. "The good people of Willow Bend haven't been very welcoming to me. I didn't want to embarrass you by speaking to you with them present."

She gripped her fingers tighter. "I'm sorry. In time, I'm sure that will change."

"That's not important today. I just wanted to make sure you're doing all right. Is there anything I can do to help you?"

She took a deep breath and forced a smile to her face. "I don't think there's anything that anyone can do at this point. My aunt is dead, my home is sold, and I'm left penniless and alone. All I can do is put my faith in God, that He will see me through this time."

"Penniless? But won't you inherit your aunt's house?"

Savannah shook her head. "Right after the war, Aunt Jane found herself with little money. My father tried to get her to come to Cottonwood and live with us, but she was very independent. She sold her house to her friend Lucas Hawkins, who is the captain of the *Montgomery Belle*. He gave her the option of living there until her death. Of course, at the time, she had no idea that I would come to live with her."

Dante leaned forward and rested his arm on the pommel of the saddle. "Do you know what you're going to do?"

"As a matter of fact, I do. When the *Montgomery Belle* docked last week on its way upriver, Captain Hawkins came to see me. He knew how sick Aunt Jane was, and he told me I could live in the house a few more years until he decided to return to Willow Bend."

"Are you going to do that?"

Savannah sighed. "There's no use prolonging the inevitable. When I said I would leave, he told me of a family in Mobile who's in need of a governess. He thought I might be interested."

Dante frowned. "A governess?"

"Yes. He said they're a very nice family with two girls. They're looking for a handyman, too, so Jasper and I have decided to go. Captain Hawkins is supposed to arrive in Willow Bend on his return journey to Mobile next week, and we plan to board the ship with him."

Dante's eyes widened in surprise. "You're going to Mobile to be a governess?"

"I don't want to leave, but I have no choice."

"B–b–but what about your friend Mr. Boyer? I assumed you would marry him."

Savannah shook her head. "Our parents wanted us to marry and join the two plantations, but I realized a long time ago that I wasn't in love with Jonathan."

The horse underneath Dante pranced, and he tightened his hold on the reins. "I hope you know I wish you the best.

Maybe I'll see you again before you leave."

"Perhaps." She held out her hand. "Thank you again for your kindness during Aunt Jane's last days and for coming today."

He gazed at her hand a moment before he reached out and grasped it in his. "It was my pleasure."

Her heart raced as he grasped her hand. Savannah pasted a big smile on her face and settled back in the buggy. "Goodbye, Mr. Rinaldi. I hope you can restore Cottonwood to what it was before the war."

He regarded her with a somber gaze. "I'll do everything in my power to make it something you'd be proud of. I promise you that."

The seat beside her sagged as Jasper sank down next to her. Turning to him, she blinked back the tears threatening to flood her eyes. "Let's go home, Jasper. We have lots to do before we leave."

Jasper snapped the reins, and the buggy moved out into the road. Savannah looked over her shoulder once. Dante Rinaldi sat on his horse staring after them. Her eyes grew wide at the sudden truth that struck her—she was going to miss him.

His words pounded in her ears. He promised he was going to make Cottonwood something she would be proud of, but she wouldn't be here to see it happen. She'd be miles away on the Gulf coast with a family she didn't know. As she'd done ever since she realized Aunt Jane was going to die, Savannah offered up a prayer.

Oh God, if there's any way possible to keep me from leaving the only place I've ever known, I pray You'll show me. If not, help me to accept what my lot will be. I put my future in Your hands.

Her heart felt lighter as she finished the prayer. She didn't know what the future held, but she knew who held her future. The faith she'd learned from her parents told her she would never be alone.

❧

Dante paced back and forth across the floor of the small cabin where he'd been living since coming to Cottonwood. From time to time, he stopped and stared into the small fire he'd built. He didn't know if the chill he felt was from cool, evening air blowing off the river or if it was caused by the turmoil within him.

Savannah was leaving in a few days, and he would never see her again. From the first moment he saw her, he hadn't been able to get her out of his mind. He'd told himself he was being silly. She hated him because she felt he had stolen her land, but that did nothing to quell the thoughts of her that ran through his head.

He began to pace again. It made no difference. He knew what was wrong with him. He was in love for the first time in his life, and it was killing him. He'd tried to lose himself in work on the plantation, but it didn't help. Every night he lay awake in this cabin, unable to shake his thoughts of Savannah.

Now she was leaving, and he was helpless to stop her.

A knock at the door startled him, and he strode across the floor. Jerking the door open, he smiled when he saw Saul and Mamie standing on the small porch. Saul pointed to the pot Mamie held. "We brung you some food, Mistuh Dante. You didn't come for supper."

He glanced at the dark sky and realized the sun had set while he was agonizing over his thoughts. He held the door open wider. "I'm sorry. That wasn't very courteous of me to ignore Mamie's fine cooking. Please forgive me."

Mamie giggled. "Land's sake, Mistuh Dante. You sho' got a

way with words. Hit ain't no trouble for us to brang this here food over to you." She set a pot on the table in the middle of the cabin. "Abraham kilt some rabbits today. So we gots good eatin' tonight."

Dante smiled, lifted the top off the pan, and sniffed. "Aw, that smells good. And you've brought me some of your good biscuits, too."

She nodded. "Thanks to you, I kin make them biscuits. We ain't seen no flour 'round here in a long time till you buy Cottonwood."

Dante motioned for them to sit. "Want to keep me company while I eat?"

Saul eyed the chairs with a skeptical look. "You wants us to sit at the table with you? That don't seem right proper, Mistuh Dante."

Dante chuckled. "And why not? I sit in your house when I eat with you. You can do the same in my house."

Saul shook his head and slipped into his seat. Mamie had already sat down at the table and was dishing out the rabbit and biscuits on a plate. "Here you goes. Now you eat up whilst we sit here and talk."

Dante's stomach growled from the aroma of the food. With a laugh, he sat down and began to devour what Mamie had brought. With the first bites, he nodded in Mamie's direction. "You're a good cook, Mamie. If I ever have a wife, you're going to have to teach her all you know."

Mamie ducked her head and grinned. A shy expression covered her face. "All I know 'bout cookin' I learnt in the kitchen at Cottonwood. Mistuh Vance and Miss Amelia used to say nobody on Cottonwood could cook like Mamie. Yas suh, that's what they said."

The mention of Savannah's parents reminded him of why

he'd missed the evening meal. He laid down his fork. "I went to the funeral of Miss Carmichael's aunt today."

Saul's eyebrows arched. "How Miss 'Vanna makin' it?"

Dante shrugged. "She looked tired, but she's had a lot to contend with in the past few weeks."

Mamie leaned forward. "What she gwine do now that her aunt done died? She gwine live in that house by herself?"

Dante picked up the fork and stabbed at a piece of meat. "No. She's leaving Willow Bend."

Saul jumped to his feet, and his chair tipped back and hit the floor with a thump. "Leavin'? Where she goin'?"

"She's moving to Mobile to be a governess to a family there. She plans to board the *Montgomery Belle* when it goes back downriver next week."

Wringing her hands, Mamie stood next to her husband. "Oh, this bad. Miss 'Vanna havin' to leave home. It just ain't right. She belongs here with us." She turned to Dante. "Ain't there somethin' you can do to make her stay?"

Dante couldn't tell Mamie that was all he'd thought about since he'd been back from the funeral. "I don't know anything I could do."

Mamie glanced up at Saul and then toward Dante. "But it just ain't right. Me and Saul think Miss 'Vanna ought to be here."

Saul grabbed his wife's arm. "Hush up, Mamie. This ain't none a' our business."

She shook her arm free. "Then whose business is it? We done saved that girl's life the night the big house burn, and we promised her we'd stay here and take care of things till she came back."

Saul shook his head. "That all changed when Mistuh Dante bought this here place."

Mamie propped her hands on her hips and frowned. "You men can't see nothin'. The day Mistuh Dante come here, I see the Lawd makin' a way for Miss 'Vanna to come home."

"What are you talking about, Mamie?" Dante asked.

Saul's eyes grew big, and he tried to steer his wife toward the door. "Don't matter. We goin' to our cabin." He glanced down at Mamie. "We can't go tellin' no white man what he ought to do. You forgettin' your place."

Dante stepped in front of them. "I thought you realized we are all equal here, Saul. If Mamie has something to say, I want to hear what it is."

Mamie straightened to her full height and sniffed. "I jest see the way you look ev'ry time you talk 'bout Miss 'Vanna. It not hard to figure out you done got struck on that girl. If you are, then you got no business lettin' her go downriver. You got to stop her and bring her home to Cottonwood."

Dante spread his hands in amazement. "And how do I do that?"

Mamie smiled. "You a smart man. You kin figure it out." She turned to Saul. "Now I 'spects we can go. Mistuh Dante gots lots of thinkin' to do."

Before he could stop them, the pair disappeared out the door, leaving him to wonder what Mamie had been insinuating. She'd said he was struck on Savannah. *Struck* was hardly the word for what he felt. He loved her with all his heart.

What could he do to bring her back to Cottonwood? She would never agree to accept his charity and live on his land. She wanted the land to belong to her again, but she had no money to purchase it. She also wanted it to pass on to her heirs. How could that be? The land would pass to his heirs.

Understanding flashed into his mind, and he sank down in the chair at the table. The only way she could have the land would be if they shared it. And it could only pass to her heirs if they shared them also.

Marriage? To him?

He shook his head and bolted to his feet. She would never agree to that. She despised him. She considered him her enemy, a person who'd stolen what she thought was rightfully hers.

Yet a marriage between the two of them made sense. Sharing Cottonwood was a small price to pay for having the woman he loved as his wife. And having a child to pass the land to would be the fulfillment of a dream he'd had for years. He would go to her tomorrow and ask her.

He covered his face with his hands and groaned. What could he say that would make her accept him as a husband?

Dante dropped to his knees beside his chair and closed his eyes. "Dear God, You know my heart. I pray You'll give me the right words as I talk with Savannah. Be with me, and give me strength as I face this crucial point in my life. Amen."

Dante rose. Almost immediately he knew what he would say to her. He'd propose a business deal. She needed a home, and she wanted Cottonwood back. He needed a wife who was respected by the community and could help him become accepted by the residents in the closed society of Willow Bend. If they married, their children would inherit the land that had been in her family for years. They both stood to gain a lot from the proposition.

Dante clapped his hands and laughed. Maybe she would say yes. He could hardly wait to find out.

seven

Savannah swallowed the last bite of her noon meal and glanced around the sparsely furnished dining room. Aunt Jane's survival since the war had depended on the money she'd received from the sale of her house and on selling off her possessions one at a time. However, there were still many items, including furniture and personal belongings, that had to go.

Savannah touched the linen tablecloth that had been one of Aunt Jane's favorites. Even when their money had dwindled to a dangerous low, it was something Aunt Jane hadn't been able to bring herself to sell. It had belonged to Savannah's grandmother, and Aunt Jane had wanted Savannah to have it when she married.

It didn't look as if that would ever happen. Her life seemed set. She would probably serve a family as governess until their children no longer needed her, then she would go to another. And so her life would be until one day she was so old that no one wanted her. Then where would she end up?

The thought sent a chill through her, and she buried her face in her hands. She had to quit thinking like this. God would take care of her. She knew that, but sometimes it was so hard to trust when the future seemed so bleak.

Sighing, she stood and walked toward the kitchen. Jasper turned from stoking the fire in the iron cookstove as she entered. A frown pulled at his face. "Miss 'Vanna, what we gwine do with all this here stuff?"

She shook her head. "I don't know, Jasper. Maybe Mr. Perkins at the store will take some of it against our account there. The eggs and butter we've sold haven't paid all of it in months."

He nodded. "Yas'm. And that reminds me. What we gwine do 'bout them chickens and the cow?"

A feeling of helplessness washed over her, and she closed her eyes. Her head hurt from all the questions that had run through her mind in the last weeks. Now she only had a few days before the *Montgomery Belle* would be back. She had to find an answer to all her problems, but she had no idea what it was.

God, she prayed, *what am I to do?*

Her eyes widened as the answer came to her, and she smiled. "I think I know what we might do with the chickens and the cow." She turned and started from the room but called over her shoulder. "Jasper, hitch the horse to the buggy. I'm going to Cottonwood. Maybe Saul and Mamie can use them since they're going to have some land of their own."

She rushed to the stairs and hurried up to her bedroom. Once in the room, she threw open the door of the big armoire that had also belonged to her grandmother. She reached for the shawl that hung on a peg but stopped.

Running her hands down the front of her simple day dress, she spied a smudge from taking out the ashes earlier in the day. She'd have to change clothes just in case she ran into the new owner of Cottonwood.

Savannah shook her head. Why was she worrying about making a good impression on Dante Rinaldi? He'd be in the fields today, and she wouldn't even see him.

Just in case, though, she reached for the blue dress with its draped skirt and ruffled jacket. They'd had to sell a lot of eggs and butter to pay for the material, but Aunt Jane had insisted that Savannah needed one fashionable dress.

Savannah pulled the dress from the armoire and crushed it against her. She'd worn this garment to Aunt Jane's funeral. Now she was going to Cottonwood in hopes of giving away some of Aunt Jane's property. If only she were going home!

She squared her shoulders and held the dress in front of her. "Quit bawling, Savannah Carmichael. God's going to take care of you. Now act like you believe it."

New resolve flowed through her. There were many things to settle before she could leave Willow Bend. One of the hardest would be to leave her parents' graves behind. Before she could say good-bye to Saul and Mamie, she had to bid her parents farewell.

Her hands tightened on the dress she held, and she buried her face in the soft material. She hoped she wouldn't see Dante Rinaldi today. Her heart told her saying good-bye to him was going to be more difficult than she'd realized.

*

Dante trudged along the path that led from the large cane-brake to the river. He'd gone alone today to that field and sent the men in other directions. He needed time alone to think and pray, although he'd done that nearly all last night. Sleep had refused to come, and he'd sat in front of the fireplace and pondered how he'd present his plan to Savannah Carmichael.

Dante ran his hand through his hair. Whatever made him come up with such an idea? All she was going to do was laugh at him and make him feel foolish. A sinking feeling hit him in the pit of his stomach. He could see his father and mother, so in love after years of marriage. That's what he'd always wanted, but he wouldn't have that even if Savannah accepted his proposal.

He clenched his fists at his side and shook his head. He was crazy to ever think he could ask her to marry him. The best thing for him to do was turn around and go back to the canebrake. Labor in that jungle of cane would drive any thoughts of the beautiful woman from his mind.

He turned to retrace his steps, but he couldn't move. It was as if some invisible hand gripped his shoulder and spun him around then nudged him forward. He remembered something else his father had once told him. *"When you think something is impossible, try it anyway."*

Dante took a deep breath. He had to try the impossible even if he regretted it later. Letting Savannah go without at least asking her would be the biggest mistake of his life.

With a new determination, he strode forward and rounded the corner to the path that led by the small cemetery. His eyes grew wide, and he came to a halt. He couldn't believe what he saw. Savannah's buggy sat in front of the cemetery gate.

Swallowing, he eased forward until he could see her. She knelt between her parents' graves, her head bowed and her lips moving in silent conversation.

His glance traveled over her. She had on the dress she'd worn to her aunt's funeral. The vision of how she'd looked in it had haunted him.

Dante stopped at the fence but didn't enter. He waited until she stood before he spoke. "Good afternoon, Miss Carmichael."

Her body stiffened, and she turned to face him. "Mr. Rinaldi. I didn't hear you approach."

"I've been in the canebrake and was on my way back home."

She walked forward and stopped inside the fence. "I came to Cottonwood to say good-bye to my parents and take care of some more business."

His eyebrows arched. "Some business? Is it anything I can help you with?"

She shook her head. "No. I'm trying to dispose of Aunt Jane's property before I leave. I thought Saul and Mamie might like to have our cow and chickens."

"That's very kind of you to think of them."

Her gaze didn't waver from his face. "Saul and Mamie are like my family. I've known them all my life." She looked up into the sky. "It's getting late. I'd better go see Mamie."

He opened the gate. "Then allow me to drive you."

"Thank you."

Dante reached out and took her arm as he assisted her into the buggy. Then he untied the reins, walked around, and climbed in beside her. Without speaking, he turned the horse and guided it back along the river.

When they approached the charred rubble of the big house, Savannah touched his arm. "Would you please stop? I want to look at it for the last time."

His heart thudded as her gaze raked the burned piles of ashes that had once been a grand house. "I saw the house the first time from a riverboat. There was a young girl on the balcony of the second floor. She waved as we passed."

Savannah smiled. "It had to be me. I used to stand out there and watch the riverboats. I knew them all." She glanced at him. "I can still tell their whistles apart."

He tightened his hands on the reins. "I'm sorry the house burned. That must have been very difficult for you."

She nodded. "I still don't know what woke me that night. I remember sitting up in bed and seeing what appeared to be slivers of moonlight dancing across my bedroom floor. But there was a glow I didn't understand. I jumped out of bed and stood in the middle of the room, trying to figure out what had awakened me."

"You must have heard the fire crackling."

"I suppose so." She hesitated a moment and then continued. "Then I felt the heat and saw the smoke. It looked like giant, licking tongues creeping underneath my bedroom door and crawling toward me. The floor was so hot that my feet burned, and I ran onto the balcony."

"What about your parents?"

Tears glimmered in her eyes. "I called them over and over, but there was no answer. The orange flames leaped from their bedroom window, and I knew I had to escape. I climbed onto the iron balustrade and screamed at the searing pain on the bottoms of my feet. I grabbed one of the hot columns and shinnied down. Saul and Mamie, along with a few former slaves who were still living in the cabins, waited at the base and helped me to the ground."

His throat constricted at the pain in her face. "But you survived."

She nodded. "Saul picked me up and carried me to their cabin, where Mamie tended my burns. The fire was so bright that it was seen all up and down the river. Some of the neighbors arrived and tried to save some part of the big house, but it was no use. In the morning, all that was left were the eight columns that still stood facing the river. Then Aunt Jane and Jasper arrived, and I left Cottonwood and all its memories behind." She glanced at him. "Do you mind if I walk around a bit for the last time?"

"Of course not," he croaked.

He climbed from the buggy and helped her down. She walked across the lawn and stopped between two of the still-standing columns. Gently she laid her hand against one of the smoke-stained pillars. Her head drooped, and his heart constricted at the horror she had faced the night of the fire.

A voice in his head whispered that this was the time for him to tell her what he'd been thinking. He tried to follow her, but his feet felt rooted to the ground.

She straightened and stared into the ruins for a moment. "After the fire, the few slaves who'd stayed on left, too, but Saul and Mamie wouldn't go. Not even after I left." She turned to him, and a tear trickled down her cheek. "Promise me that someday a house will stand on this spot."

Unable to stand seeing her in pain any longer, he forced his feet to move. He stopped behind her. "I promise." He took a deep breath. "Miss Carmichael, there's something I'd like to talk to you about."

She wiped at her eyes. "What is it?"

A declaration of how much he loved her hovered on the tip of his tongue, but he knew to utter it would be a terrible mistake. He had to make his proposition appeal to her, and love from an Italian that she equated with a carpetbagger wouldn't do.

He cleared his throat. "I know a way you can stay in Willow Bend."

She shook her head. "No, Mr. Rinaldi. I have nothing in Willow Bend to keep me there."

Perspiration popped out on his head. "I didn't make myself clear. I'm not talking about the town of Willow Bend. I'm talking about Cottonwood."

Her eyebrows drew down into a frown. "I don't understand."

He ignored the trickle of sweat that ran down his cheek. "I know you love Cottonwood and you blame me for taking it away from you. But let me ask you this: How far would you go to get Cottonwood back?"

Her eyes narrowed. "That's a question that has no answer,

because I don't have any money, and I would do nothing illegal to regain my home."

He raked his hand through his hair. He was saying this all wrong. "I don't mean anything against the law. Would you be willing to enter into a business proposition if you could regain Cottonwood?"

Savannah sighed. "Get to the point, Mr. Rinaldi. I have no idea what you're talking about."

"All right, I will. But please hear me out before you answer. I've been thinking about your predicament. Your life has taken a sad turn since the war ended. Your father let Cottonwood fail, and you were unable to stop the tax collectors. Now you're going off to work as a governess." He stepped closer. "You aren't the kind of woman who works for another family. You belong here on the land your family farmed."

"And how do I do that?"

He took a deep breath. "By marrying me."

Her mouth gaped open, and her eyes grew wide. She staggered back a step from him. "Marry you? Have you lost your mind?"

He shook his head. "I told you to hear me out. If you became my wife, the land would in essence be yours again. You could run our home and help manage the tenant farmers and whatever else you wanted to do. I would never refer to it again as my land."

A look of disbelief covered her face. "I can't believe you're serious."

"I assure you I am."

She turned away for a moment and then faced him. "And just what do you get out of this business deal?"

"I find I'm an outsider in the community. I want to be accepted by other families, and by marrying you, I figure I have a way of making that happen. Besides, I need a wife because I want Cottonwood to pass to my children, too."

"This is insane," she whispered. "We don't love each other."

Her words sliced his heart like a knife. "You may not love me, but you love the land. Why not marry me to get it back?"

She studied him for a moment. "That's a good point, Mr. Rinaldi. There is one more thing, though. What about Jasper?"

Dante shrugged. "Jasper can come to Cottonwood, too, if he wants. There's always room for one more. And if you agree to marry me, I'll have Saul and the other tenant farmers help me move everything from your aunt's house here. We can store her things until I get a better house built for you."

Tears puddled in her eyes. "I wouldn't have to sell Aunt Jane's possessions, Jasper can come to Cottonwood, and I'll have my land back. You'll do all that just to be accepted by a community of snobs who are still fighting the war?"

He longed to tell her that he would do it all and more just for her. "Yes, and who knows. We may come to love each other, but even if you never love me, I hope you can respect me as a person."

She turned, took a few steps, and stood unmoving. After a moment, her tense body relaxed, and she faced him. "This is all so sudden. I—I don't know what to say."

He tried to ignore the hope that burned in his heart. "If you need more time, I'll understand. This is a big decision. The question you must answer is what do you want: to be a governess in Mobile or to be the mistress of your family's land."

Her lips parted, and she exhaled. "When you put it that way, Mr. Rinaldi, there's only one choice. I accept your proposal."

The breath left his body as if he'd been kicked in the

stomach. He'd been prepared for her to scream how crazy he was for thinking she would even consider marriage with such a ridiculous Italian as he. Instead, she uttered the words that made him the happiest he'd ever been. He struggled to keep his excitement from showing.

"Thank you for doing me the honor of becoming my wife. I promise I will take care of you. I don't want you to suffer anymore hurts like the past."

She smiled. "Beneath your rough exterior, Mr. Rinaldi, I think there is a very kind person. Thank you for bringing me home."

He swallowed at the sincerity in her voice. "When would you like to have the ceremony?"

"How about tomorrow?"

Dante gasped. "So soon? But I don't have a place for you to stay yet. I'm living in one of the slave quarters. You can't stay there."

"If it's on Cottonwood's land, I can stay anywhere. I'll go back to town and talk with Reverend Somers about performing the ceremony tomorrow afternoon. If it's all right with you, we can stay at Aunt Jane's tomorrow night and start moving my things the next day." She stopped and frowned. "Unless you'd rather wait."

He shook his head. "No, no. It just surprised me that you would want to do it so quickly."

"I want to do this before I have time to convince myself this is all wrong. I've been obsessed with coming back home. The sooner I'm here, the better."

"Then I will go to your aunt's house in the early afternoon tomorrow and escort you to the church."

She nodded. "Will you bring anyone with you to witness the marriage?"

He searched his mind. He knew no one except the people at Cottonwood. "I suppose I could bring one of the tenant farmers."

"Don't worry about it. I'll ask Mrs. Somers and my friend Sarah Morgan. That should be enough." She reached for the reins. "I suppose that's all we need to discuss. I shall expect you tomorrow then."

He nodded, still unable to believe what had just happened. "I'll be there."

Dante watched until her buggy disappeared from view before he turned and hurried toward his cabin. His feet almost skimmed the surface of the ground. All day he'd been telling himself he was being foolish to even think about asking Savannah Carmichael to marry him. But she had said yes.

He ran onto the porch of his cabin and burst through the door. Inside he stopped and looked around at the place where he would bring her. It wasn't what he wanted for her, but for now, it was the best he could do.

Take one step at a time—that's what he had to do. First, he had to make her his wife, and then everything else would fall into place. They could have a good life together, even if she didn't love him. He could be happy just having her near.

&

Savannah's mind raced as she rode back to town. What would her friends think when they heard she had married the man who bought Cottonwood? No doubt many of them would denounce her for joining herself to an outsider and accuse her of doing wrong.

Right now she couldn't think about right and wrong. All she knew was that the man whose dark eyes made her heart race had given her a chance to come home, and that's what she wanted.

Dante was handsome and a hard worker. He was also kind. She'd seen that the first day they met, although she hadn't wanted to acknowledge it then. His attention to Aunt Jane over the past month had shown her his gentle nature. Yes, she could do a lot worse in a husband. But the good thing about the whole arrangement was she'd be back at Cottonwood.

It would be different. She wouldn't be Savannah Carmichael anymore. She would have the strange name of Rinaldi. A smile curled her lips. Savannah Rinaldi. She liked the sound of it.

eight

"Savannah, we're back at your aunt's house."

The soft voice penetrated the silence that had hung over her and Dante on their return from the church. While she'd been lost in thought, Dante had climbed from the buggy and waited to assist her.

She stared at Dante. Was he really her husband? Perhaps the last hour had been a dream. Her gaze traveled to the gold band that circled the fourth finger of her left hand.

"It was my mother's."

Savannah frowned and glanced at Dante. "What?"

He cleared his throat. "The ring. It was my mother's. After she died, I knew I wanted my wife to wear it someday."

She flinched at the strange sensation stirring within her. "And now it's mine."

"Yes." The word was little more than a whisper.

This was no dream. Everything had changed with her visit to Cottonwood yesterday. *"For better or worse,"* Reverend Somers had said, and now they were joined for life.

Savannah swallowed the fear that knotted her stomach and tried to smile. "I will try to be worthy of wearing your mother's ring."

"I'm sure you will." He held out his hand again. "Now are you ready to go inside? I imagine there's a lot to do before Saul and the men come from Cottonwood tomorrow."

She slipped her hand into his and stepped to the ground. The pressure of his fingers on hers tightened, but she pulled away once she stood next to him. "Thank you."

"I'll put the horse away and then come inside."

Before she could protest that Jasper liked to see to the horse himself, the man appeared from around the corner of the house. His mouth pulled into a big smile when he saw them. He stopped next to the horse and rested his hand on the mare's back. "Miss 'Vanna, Mistuh Dante, you done got married already?"

"Yes." They spoke at the same time.

"I bet that cer'mony was somethin' to see. Miss 'Vanna, you a purty bride."

Dante nodded. "That she is."

His words surprised her. Did he mean it, or was he just being courteous?

Savannah bit her lip and looked at the ground. Her face burned. How was she supposed to act? A glance at him told her he probably felt the same way.

One's wedding day was supposed to be one of the happiest days of one's life, but hers had been forged out of a need for acceptance in the community and a desire for land. All the time Reverend Somers was reading the words, her mind had whirled with one question—how could this ever work? They were too different. She had grown up in a gentle society that believed life would go on forever in the South as it had for years. The war had put an end to that notion.

He, on the other hand, had been raised in a family who came from a foreign land and worked hard to make a new life in America. Dante had bought Cottonwood with the fruits of their long hours of labor. All he knew was work. At least they had that in common.

She looked back at Jasper, who seemed to be waiting for her to answer. "Yes, Jasper, it was a very nice ceremony." She took a deep breath. "Dante said he'd take care of the horse."

Jasper shook his head and untied the reins from the hitching post. "No'm. I'll do it. It just rightly seems my job."

Savannah regarded the man she'd known since childhood. Her heart lurched at the thought of Aunt Jane and how she would react to what was happening to both her and Jasper now. "Jasper, I wish you would reconsider and come to Cottonwood with us."

Jasper took off the hat he wore and wiped at the sweat on his brow. "I been free a long time, Miss 'Vanna. Miss Jane done give me my freedom a long time 'fore the war and tole me I could go anywhere I wanted, but I jest didn't want to leave home. But now she gone, and Mistuh Dante gwine take care of you. So I reckon it's time."

"But where will you go? What will you do?"

Jasper stared past her, and his eyes held a faraway look as if he were envisioning sights he'd never encountered. "I always had me a hankerin' to see the ocean 'fore I die. So I guess I'll get on the *Belle* when Captain Hawkins comes back, and I'll go on down to Mobile."

Tears welled in her eyes. "I'll worry about you."

Jasper chuckled. "I be all right."

"Well then, I'll give you what little money I have. I've saved up some from the eggs and butter we've sold."

Jasper shook his head. "Ain't no need for that. Mistuh Dante done give me money."

The words shocked her, and she turned to stare at Dante, who had remained silent during her exchange with Jasper. "When did you do that?"

Dante's face flushed. "I talked to Jasper when I came to take you to the church. I asked him to come to Cottonwood with us, but he told me about his plans. So I gave him some money."

Savannah stared at the man she had just married. When she'd first met him, she had thought she hated him and was sure he would always be her enemy. In the weeks since, she had come to see kindness in him. She wondered what other surprises awaited her as she got to know her husband even better.

"That was very kind of you, Dante. I appreciate all you've done for those I love."

He smiled and turned back to Jasper. "I hope you get to see the ocean, Jasper, but if things don't go the way you want, remember you always have a home at Cottonwood."

Jasper clutched his hat to his chest and nodded. "Thank you, Mistuh Dante."

Dante took a deep breath and grasped her arm. "Now, my dear, are you ready to go inside?"

Her skin tingled at his touch, and she pulled away. "Yes."

On the porch, she fumbled with the door latch, and he reached around her to open it. "Allow me."

"Thank you."

They stepped into the entry, and Savannah headed to the parlor. Once inside, she stopped in the middle of the room in confusion. Should she sit or stand? If she sat on the sofa, he might sit next to her, and she didn't want to be that near him right now. Unsure of what to do, she waited until he entered. Then she turned to face him. His eyes clouded, and he stopped in front of her.

"I know a lot has happened since yesterday, and you may be wondering why you ever agreed to my proposal. But however you feel about me, I want you to know one thing." He paused. "Savannah, you don't have to be afraid of me."

She tried to laugh, but the sound stuck in her throat. "A—afraid?"

He tilted his head. "Don't look at me like you're a rabbit that the dogs have cornered. This isn't going to be easy for either of us, but we need to come to some kind of understanding right now."

She backed away from him. "What kind of understanding?"

He took a deep breath. "I will never force you to do anything that makes you uncomfortable. Do you understand?"

Her face burned, but she forced herself to meet his gaze. "Yes."

"The cabin is small. Right now there is only one bedroom. I've been sleeping there, but I will let you have the bed."

Her eyes grew wide. "But where will you sleep?"

"In the main room on the floor." He chuckled. "I've slept in worse places in my life, and a pallet on the floor by a fire doesn't sound all that bad to me."

She nodded. "You're very kind to respect my feelings, and I appreciate it."

He took a step toward her. "We both grew up with parents who loved each other. We may not have what our parents had between them, but we have something else."

"What?"

"We saw how they respected and treated each other. I promise that I will respect you and be kind to you. I will always protect you and see that your needs are met. And when the time comes that you feel comfortable with me being your husband in every way, don't be afraid to tell me. After all, we both want an heir."

The sincerity in his face told her he meant what he said. Peace flowed through her troubled mind and replaced the uneasiness she'd felt moments ago. Perhaps her life with Dante was going to be all right after all.

"Thank you, Dante. I promise that I will respect you. And

thank you for giving me some time to adjust to being your wife. I will also do everything I can to make you accepted by the community."

He smiled. "Then I would say we're starting our marriage with more than many couples have."

She nodded. "I suppose we are."

His gaze raked her face and lingered on her lips. He moved closer, and she tilted her face up and closed her eyes. Her heart thudded as she awaited his kiss.

Disappointment flowed through her at the touch of his lips grazing her cheek. "I'm honored to have you as my wife."

She opened her eyes and stared up into his face. Before she could speak, the front door burst open, and footsteps pounded across the hallway.

"Savannah! Where are you?" Jonathan's angry voice pierced her ears.

She stepped around Dante as Jonathan rushed into the room. He cast a look of pure hatred in Dante's direction before he grabbed Savannah by the shoulders. "Tell me it's not true!"

Savannah tried to pull away from him, but Jonathan held her fast. "Jonathan, what's the matter?"

"Tell me you didn't marry this foreigner," he yelled.

Savannah wriggled in his grasp, but his hands clamped down harder. "Jonathan, let me go."

"No! You can't do this to me."

Dante appeared at her side and grabbed Jonathan's arm. She glanced around and quaked at the dark anger lining Dante's face. "Take your hands off my wife," he muttered.

Jonathan let go, and Dante stepped in front of her. His hands were clenched at his side, and his tense body told Savannah he was ready to strike out. She moved to Dante's side and faced Jonathan.

"It's true, Jonathan. Dante and I were married this afternoon. I'm sorry I didn't tell you, but it all happened so quickly."

Jonathan shook his head as if he couldn't believe what he was hearing. His body sagged, and he regarded her with stricken eyes. "Why, Savannah? How could you have done such a thing?"

"I know what I'm doing. Dante has offered me a home at Cottonwood, and I agreed."

Jonathan's face hardened as if a mask covered it. The hatred he'd directed at Dante when he entered now focused on her. "So you betrayed your parents for a piece of land."

She shrank away from him. "My parents? What do you mean?"

He leaned toward her, but he glanced at Dante and straightened. "You know your father meant for me to have that land, but you've taken it away from me by marrying this carpetbagger."

Next to her, Dante shook with rage. "Now listen to me—"

She laid her hand on his arm. "No, Dante. Let me handle this." She faced Jonathan. "Whatever our parents planned for us was a long time ago. You know there was no way Cottonwood was ever going to be mine again. I had no money, just like everyone else around here. I'm sorry if you think I've betrayed you, but you never offered me any options. Thanks to Dante, I have a home again."

"You could have had a home at Oak Hill."

She reached out and touched Jonathan's arm. "It doesn't matter now. I'm married to Dante."

Jonathan shook free of her grasp. Backing away, he pointed his finger at them. "This isn't over. You've made me a laughingstock in front of all our friends. You'll be sorry."

He whirled and ran from the room. Savannah hurried after him. "Jonathan, come back here."

By the time she got to the front door, he was already on his horse and galloping away. Tears stood in her eyes as she remembered the boy she'd known all her life. The angry man she'd just encountered wasn't the same person. But then, most of the people she knew were different. The war had taken its toll on all of them.

She felt Dante's presence behind her. "I'm sorry about your friend, Savannah."

"It doesn't matter. I don't know Jonathan anymore."

She wiped at the corner of her eye before she closed the door and turned around. He stared at her, and she let her gaze drop to the floor. "I suppose I should get supper started, but I need to change clothes first. Why don't you and Jasper look at the tools in Aunt Jane's smokehouse? You can decide what you want to take with us."

"All right." He pointed to the small valise he'd left sitting in the hallway before they went to the church. "I'll need to change also. Where should I do that?"

She glanced toward the stairs. "My bedroom is to the right at the top of the landing. Go on and get settled in there. I'll change after you're through."

His shoulders sagged as he mounted the stairs, and she wondered if Jonathan's anger had caused Dante to have second thoughts about marrying her. She raised her left hand and gazed at the gold band once more. If he was having second thoughts, it was too late now.

The enormity of what she'd done hit her, and her eyes widened. It was one thing to talk about marrying Dante so she could go home. It was quite different when she remembered the vows made before God.

She glanced up the stairs. Dante had stopped halfway up and was studying her as she stared at his mother's ring. A frown wrinkled his brow before he inhaled and continued to the second floor. Savannah let her hand drop to her side and stared at him until he disappeared into her bedroom.

Dante's words about her not being afraid of him flashed through her mind, and the truth hit her like a kick in the stomach. She feared Dante less than anyone she'd ever known. Peace flowed into her heart, and she smiled. Working together, they might be able to return Cottonwood to what it had once been, but they might also be able to build a good life.

❧

Dante set the valise on the floor in Savannah's bedroom and looked around. The quilt on the bed looked worn, but he could tell it had once been an elegant coverlet. The curtains at the window also appeared to have been in use for a long time. The house's furnishings reflected the lifestyle of a bygone era—both frayed and tattered by a war that tore a nation apart.

A walnut dresser with Savannah's personal items on top sat against one wall. He gazed at the brush with a tarnished silver handle. Golden hair clung to the bristles. He picked it up and turned it slowly in his hand.

His heart had almost stopped when Jonathan told her she could have had a home at Oak Hill and she replied she didn't know that. If Jonathan had spoken earlier, Savannah might very well have married him. Dante gripped the brush tighter. Savannah was his wife now, and he was going to do everything in his power to make her happy.

She might never love him, but perhaps she could become content to live with him at Cottonwood. Only time would tell.

nine

Savannah could hardly believe that nearly four months had passed since her marriage, but all she had to do was look at the world around her to see the passing of time. Summer green had turned to autumn, which gave way to winter. The scarlet leaves of the dogwoods that lined the edge of Cottonwood's forests now lay mingled on the woodland floor with the brilliant gold from the hickory trees she loved. Most days woodpeckers could be heard hammering at the hardwoods, but there was only silence today. Maybe they were resting, too, on the Sabbath.

A chilling breeze rustled the bare limbs of the trees on either side of the road. Savannah pulled her coat tighter against the cold morning air and snuggled back into the buggy's seat. Beside her, Dante guided the horse along the bumpy road that led to Willow Bend.

Savannah glanced at her handsome husband and pulled the buggy robe over her legs.

Dante gripped the reins with one hand and reached over to tuck the heavy covering more securely around her. "Is that better?" The slight smile she'd come to know in the months since their marriage played at his lips.

She nodded. "Yes. Thank you."

He turned his attention back to the horse and took a deep breath. "I love crisp mornings like this. When January comes, I know it won't be long until we can be in the fields and getting ready for planting."

"I know."

In the days since their marriage, they had developed a comfortable relationship. Most of their conversations centered on the land, spring planting, and the new house they would have before next fall, but that hadn't been a bad thing. All in all, she and Dante had gotten off to a good start. He and the men worked hard all day, and he came home exhausted at night. No matter how tired he was, he always had time to listen to her day's activities. Sometimes when she talked, his penetrating gaze would bore into her and take her breath away.

It was times like that when she dreamed of romance. She supposed every girl wanted to be swept off her feet, but for her it hadn't been that way. Now as she got to know Dante better, she had begun to wish for something more in their relationship.

She sensed he was watching her, and she turned to meet his gaze. "What are you looking at in the woods?" he asked.

"Nothing really, and then again everything." She laughed at the absurdity of her remark. "I'm remembering the beautiful colors of fall that are gone and enjoying the winter landscape." She pointed to the forest. "I thought the color of the leaves this year was the most beautiful I'd ever seen."

He smiled and flicked the reins across the horse's back. "Maybe next year you'll walk with me and show me your favorite spots."

Savannah's heart thudded, and she looked at him. Her mouth felt like cotton. She tried to answer, but the words wouldn't come. Before she could recover, the churchyard with buggies and wagons scattered about came into view.

She straightened in her seat. "It doesn't look like a very big crowd today."

Dante guided the horse into the churchyard and pulled to

a stop. He jumped down, tied the reins to a tree, and walked around to face her. Extending his hand, he smiled. "Let's see if the local residents are any happier to see me today than they've been in the past."

She gripped his hand and stepped to the ground. "I've told you to be patient. I thought last Sunday several more people spoke to you."

He chuckled. "I suppose you can say that. I thought I never would get away from Martha Thompson, but I had the feeling her conversation was more to find out something she could repeat to the townspeople the next day."

Savannah laughed. "I think you're probably right, but I—"

A loud voice rang out. "Savannah!"

She and Dante spied Jonathan Boyer at the same moment. Dante tensed as Jonathan pulled his horse to a stop in front of them. Jonathan glared at Dante.

"Jonathan," she said, "I'm glad to see you've finally come to church."

He shook his head and climbed down from the horse. "I'm not here for services. I wanted to see you."

Dante stepped closer to Savannah. "I hope you know you're welcome to visit Savannah anytime at Cottonwood, Mr. Boyer."

Jonathan's lip curled into a sneer. "As if I'd set foot on ground you stole."

Dante's fists clenched, and he sucked in his breath. Savannah laid a restraining hand on her husband's arm. "Please, Dante, let's not have a scene in the churchyard. Why don't you go on inside? I'll be right along."

He stared at her. "I don't think you need to talk to him. I don't trust him."

She waved her hand in dismissal. "Don't be ridiculous. I've

known Jonathan all my life. I'm perfectly safe with him."

Dante hesitated for a moment before he bit his lip and nodded. "All right. If that's the way you want it."

He whirled around and strode across the yard. Savannah swallowed back the impulse to run after him. He looked as if her words had hurt him, and she didn't want that. She turned back to Jonathan. "Now what do you want?"

Jonathan rubbed the horse's reins that he held. "Savannah, I've been miserable these last few months. I can't believe what has happened to us."

"I'm afraid I don't understand, Jonathan."

He swallowed, and Savannah detected moisture in his eyes. His shoulders slumped. "Please forgive me. I should have helped you more. Ever since the war, I've been so obsessed with getting Oak Hill back to what it was I forgot what our parents wanted. I should have figured out a way to get Cottonwood back."

She reached out and grasped his hand. "You can't blame yourself for what has happened."

"But I do. Even when I knew you were about to leave, I did nothing. I stood back and let another man take what was rightfully mine."

Savannah gasped. "Cottonwood was never yours to have, Jonathan."

He shook his head. "I'm not talking about the plantation. I'm talking about you. I let that man take you away from me, and I did nothing. I should have married you."

Tears came to her eyes, and she wiped at them. "Don't torture yourself like this. It wasn't meant for us to marry. You didn't love me, and I don't love you."

He gritted his teeth and glanced at the church. "And do you love him?"

His question stunned her. She'd barely known Dante when they married, and now she realized he was one of the kindest men she'd ever met. She respected him, but love had never been spoken between them. After four months of marriage, he was still sleeping in the main room, but he'd never complained. Still, she couldn't deny the pleasure she received when his gaze swept over her or the way her heart thudded when she looked into his eyes.

She took a deep breath and spoke. "He's my husband."

Jonathan dropped the horse's reins and grabbed both her arms. "Answer me. Do you love him?"

From behind her, a voice called out. "Take your hands off my wife!"

She turned to see Dante charging across the yard. Jonathan let go of her and tensed. Before he could step around her, she grabbed his arms. "Jonathan, please don't cause any trouble here. Get on your horse and leave before something bad happens." He glanced down at her, and uncertainty lined his face.

"Please, go. Now."

He grabbed the reins and swung into the saddle just before Dante reached them. "I'm leaving, but you haven't seen the last of me." He glared at Dante and then Savannah. "I didn't think I'd ever see the day when a Southern woman would turn her back on her people for a yellow coward who wouldn't even fight in the war. You deserve each other."

Jonathan pulled back on the right rein and dug his leg into the horse's right side. The horse turned and galloped away. Savannah watched him disappear. Jonathan had never been the same after the war, but his behavior today bordered on insanity. He was one of the living victims of the war, and she had no idea how to help him.

Fighting back tears, she turned to Dante. "Thank you for coming back."

"I was afraid he was going to hurt you."

She took a deep breath. "Let's go inside. I don't want anybody to know what happened here today."

As they walked beside each other on their way to the church, Savannah was very mindful of her husband's presence. When Jonathan asked her if she loved Dante, she hadn't answered, and she wondered what had kept her from speaking. Could it be that Dante had come to mean more to her than she realized?

When they reached the church entrance, Dante grasped her arm to assist her up the steps. She glanced at him, and the look in his dark eyes sent a ripple of pleasure through her. In his gaze, she detected the unspoken promise that he would always be her protector.

Her heart swelled, and she stepped closer to him. The truth that she'd put out of her mind for the past few months wouldn't be ignored any longer. She didn't know when it had happened, but she had fallen completely in love with her husband.

❧

Dante could hardly concentrate on the sermon. His mind whirled with what had happened earlier. When Jonathan had grabbed Savannah, Dante thought he would go mad. He couldn't stop himself from charging back.

He had no idea what they had said to each other, but whatever it was, it had upset her. The look on her pale face made his muscles contract. When she'd become his wife, he promised himself he would protect her and take care of her as long as he lived. For him, there would never be another woman. He'd started to tell her many times how he felt, but he still hadn't brought himself to do that. Maybe he would soon.

With a start, he realized that the congregation had stood. He jumped to his feet and joined in the closing hymn. After the "Amen," he grabbed Savannah's arm and steered her from the church before any of the church members could stop them.

When they were in the buggy and on their way home, he could stand it no longer. "Are you going to tell me what Boyer said to you?"

She sighed. "It was just a repeat of past conversations. He feels like he lost what was his."

"Cottonwood?"

"Yes." She paused. "And me."

The words sliced through Dante. "You said your parents had planned for you to marry, but you never said you wanted it."

She sat up straighter. "I didn't. I think Jonathan feels like he lost some kind of battle, and he can't accept it."

"I suppose I'm his enemy for all time."

"I hope not. Jonathan was once a fun-loving young man. He was a wonderful son and brother—and a great friend. The war changed the person I knew."

Dante nodded. "It changed a lot of people."

"Why. . .why. . . ?" She hesitated and cleared her throat.

Dante glanced at Savannah. Her knuckles whitened from her clenched hands on top of the buggy robe. "What were you going to ask?"

She took a deep breath. "Why didn't you fight in the war?"

The memories he'd struggled to erase surged into his mind. "Why do you ask?"

"Because you were the right age to enlist, yet you didn't. How did you get out of going when everybody else was being drafted?"

He took the reins in one hand and rubbed the other over his eyes. "I've never spoken about that to anyone, but maybe it's time I did." He paused for a moment, wondering where to begin. "When I was young, my father worked for a landowner named Thomas Jackson. He had a big plantation near Mobile. He didn't own any slaves, just worked his land with hired men. I helped out, too, and he took a liking to me. In 1855, when I was fourteen, my parents died of yellow fever. I didn't have any family, so Mr. Jackson let me live with him."

"He sounds like a nice man."

"He was. When the war came, I told him I would run away before I stepped on a battlefield and killed men who were trying to free the slaves. He understood my feelings and told me he'd try to help. He knew the people involved in conscripting soldiers, and he begged my case before them. As a favor to him, they agreed to exempt me from serving as a soldier if I would work as a medical helper on the battlefield."

Savannah's eyes grew wide. "What did you do?"

"I agreed. Saving lives instead of taking them seemed the right thing to do."

"Then why do you tell people you didn't serve in the war?"

"Because they ask the question meaning, did I fight? and no, I didn't bear arms against another man. But the fight I had was probably as difficult as facing death."

Her forehead wrinkled. "What kind of fight did you have?"

"The doctors, officers, and even some of the wounded didn't like the idea of what they considered a coward helping them. I got the dirtiest jobs in the field hospitals and took the most abuse, but I survived. And now I can face those families living on Cottonwood and know that I didn't fight to keep them enslaved."

"What did you do after the war?"

"I went back to Mr. Jackson and worked for him. He'd kept my money safe, and he paid me a lot more after the war. When he died, his brother inherited the land, but Mr. Jackson left me a large sum of money that helped me to buy Cottonwood."

She sat in thought for a moment before she spoke. "The war changed all our lives, didn't it? I can't imagine what it must have been like for you. I admire you for being true to your beliefs. Thank you for telling me."

He nodded and directed his attention back to the horse. He hadn't ever meant to tell her about that. And he hadn't related how horrible it had been in those battlefield hospitals. He'd never forget all he'd seen.

Perhaps he should have kept those memories to himself. He wanted her to judge him on what he was now, not what he'd been years ago. His story very well could convince her that he was a coward. If she believed that, it would be even worse than what he'd endured on the battlefield.

ten

Savannah had tried all afternoon to erase the vision of Jonathan's angry face from her mind. She could still see how he'd looked when he called her and Dante his enemies. He didn't mean it, she told herself. She'd talk to him soon, and everything would be all right.

When she wasn't thinking about Jonathan, she thought about Dante's revelation about his war experiences. She'd never known another man who had gone to such extremes to stand up for his convictions. When he could have run away or even gone north to fight, he chose to accept a gruesome existence in a battlefield hospital. She could only imagine the horror he'd endured amid the hurt and dying.

Her heart swelled with pride for her husband's actions. If the people of Willow Bend only knew, she was sure they would accept him. However, it was his story, not hers, to tell, and she would never breach his confidence.

The door to the cabin opened, and Dante stepped in. He closed the door, pulled off his gloves, and blew on his hands. "It's getting colder. I wouldn't doubt if it gets down to freezing tonight."

Savannah hurried across the room that served as their combination parlor, kitchen, and dining room and grabbed the back of his coat as he shrugged it from his shoulders. "Freezing? It hardly ever gets that cold here."

She hung his coat on the peg next to the door. When she turned, he was staring at her. "Thank you."

Puzzled, she frowned. "For what?"

"For helping me with my coat."

Her face burned, and she pointed toward the iron cook-stove they'd brought from Aunt Jane's house. "I've got a good fire going. Scoot your chair up and get warm while I finish supper."

As he settled in the chair, she turned her attention back to the pots on the stove. "Did you get all the livestock watered?"

"Yes, thanks to Abraham and Joshua. Saul and Mamie have two mighty fine sons. They're some of the best workers I've ever seen."

Savannah replaced the lid on the pot she'd just checked. "They are. Abraham is a little older than me, and Joshua is younger. Mamie used to make us sit while she was scrubbing clothes, and she'd tell us stories. I always thought Abraham was so funny. He loved to laugh and make jokes. I thought he might leave when he got his freedom, but he hasn't."

Dante shrugged. "I think he loves his parents too much to leave. And now there's someone else. A young girl named Hattie. She lives at the Crossroads. Her family hasn't found a place to work yet."

"Maybe they'll find something soon." Dante's face flushed, and she knew it wasn't from the heat of the stove. "What is it? Is there something you haven't told me?"

"Abraham really wants to marry Hattie. So we decided Saul and Mamie's house needed an extra room. He and Hattie can live there for a while. After next year's crop, I think we'll be able to set Abraham up with his own acreage to farm."

Savannah placed her hands on her hips and gazed at her husband. Every day he surprised her with something else he did for the people she'd loved all her life. "You're a kind man, Dante Rinaldi. In the short time I've known you, you've done more for me and those I love than anyone else ever has. Thank you for that."

His gaze raked her face. "I appreciate that, Savannah." He glanced down at his hands and held them out toward the warmth of the stove. "I've been meaning to ask you if you're upset because we're going to build Saul and Mamie's house before ours."

She frowned. "No. Why would you think I'd be upset?"

His gaze traveled around the walls of the small cabin that had once housed slaves. "I know this isn't where you imagined yourself living, and I will build us a better house. But the roof on Saul and Mamie's cabin is the worst on the plantation. I wanted them to have something better first."

"I understand. Our house will come later."

He nodded. "Yes, our house."

The way he said the words sent tremors through her body. Savannah pulled her gaze away from him and reached for the iron skillet that hung on the wall. Her hands shook as she placed it on top of the stove and placed the pieces of ham she'd cut earlier in it.

Dante rose from his chair and moved to stand behind her. As he peered over her shoulder, she could feel his breath on her neck, and it sent ripples up and down her back. "Um, this looks good. Ham and biscuits?"

"Yes. I haven't made the biscuits yet, but I made your favorite—fried peach pies."

He moved closer. "Who taught you how to cook?"

She took a deep breath. "Mamie cooked for us in the big house. My mother didn't know the first thing about the kitchen, but I stayed there a lot. All that I learned came from Mamie."

He chuckled. "Then I owe Mamie a great debt of gratitude."

"That's almost the last of the ham we brought from Aunt Jane's smokehouse, though. Do you think we'll be able to butcher some hogs soon?"

He stepped back to his chair and sat down. "I'll see if I can buy a few from one of the farmers. By next year, though, we'll be able to fill each family's smokehouse."

Savannah glanced over her shoulder at him. "Mamie and I are already talking about the garden we're going to plant in the spring. With the help of all the women, we should be able to grow enough vegetables to get us through next winter. We'll have to take a look at the apple and peach orchards, though. They've been neglected for a long time."

Dante stared at her for a moment, and she thought she detected respect in his eyes. "You surprise me, Savannah."

She frowned. "How?"

"You cook, you're ready to butcher hogs, and you're already planning next spring's garden. I expect you'll have us all out in the orchard pruning and doing whatever it takes to get those trees producing again. I wouldn't have thought a beautiful woman who grew up the pampered daughter of a planter would do those things."

She snorted. "Then you have a lot to learn about me. I told you I wanted to bring Cottonwood back to what it was before the war, and I meant it." She stopped and bit her lip. "Which reminds me, there is one more thing I've been meaning to mention."

"What?"

Savannah took a deep breath. She had no idea how he would respond to her next suggestion. She wiped her hands on her apron and faced him. "I know you've been concerned about transporting our baled cotton next year to Willow Bend to load on the steamboats going to Mobile."

He nodded. "Yes. There doesn't seem to be a good place to build a steamboat landing. The bluffs along the river on our land are too steep. It'll take a lot of time to take the cotton to Willow Bend by wagon."

"I have an idea. What if we built a slide from the top of the bluff straight down to the water? There's a good place at the bottom of the bluff near that canebrake you and the men cleaned out where the ship could dock. Some of the men could push the bales straight down to the ship, and others could be at the bottom to load it. That would eliminate the need to take it into Willow Bend."

"Savannah, I said a few minutes ago that you surprise me, but that's not correct. You amaze me."

A quizzical expression lined his face, and she felt a pang of regret. He looked at her as if she'd lost her mind. He must think her a silly woman to come up with such an idea.

Her face burned. "It's just a suggestion. If you don't like it, I'm sure you'll come up with something else." She turned back to the stove.

His hands touched her shoulders, and she froze in place. Turning her to face him, he smiled. "Not like it? I think it's a brilliant idea. I didn't realize what a keen mind you have."

Her uncertainty melted away, and she smiled back at him. "You really like the idea?"

"I love it. Saul told me that even though you were a young girl you could have run the plantation after the war. I think if you had, things might be different." He'd no sooner said it than his eyes clouded. "And you wouldn't have had to marry me."

He released his hold on her, and she felt chilled. The breath caught in her throat. "I didn't have to marry you, Dante. I'm glad I did."

His Adam's apple bobbed. "Are you really glad, Savannah?"

She cupped his hand in both of hers. "You're a good man, Dante, and I'm honored to be your wife."

He smiled. "No, I'm the one who is honored." He turned away and disappeared into the bedroom. In a few minutes, he returned, his Bible in his hand. Without speaking, he sat at the kitchen table, opened it, and began to read.

The ham in the skillet sizzled, and Savannah turned her attention back to the meal. She stole a glance every once in a while over her shoulder, but Dante didn't look up. Something about the sight of him sitting there, studying God's Word warmed her heart. Every day she found another reason to respect and like her husband. She wondered what he thought about her.

&

Dante tried to concentrate on the scripture, but he found it difficult. Savannah's presence in the room distracted him. The words she'd spoken a few minutes earlier made it almost impossible to think about anything else except her.

He glanced up and studied her as she put the last touches on their evening meal. He still couldn't believe that she was his wife, but here she was. His prayers of thanks were offered each day for God blessing him in such a way. Maybe he should tell her how he felt—let her know how dear she was to him.

A knock at the door startled him, and he jumped to his feet. "I'll get it."

When he opened the door, Abraham, Saul and Mamie's older son, stood on the porch. He held something covered with a cloth in one hand. Dante opened the door wider.

"Abraham, come in."

The young man stepped into the room and grinned. His ebony skin glistened in the light from the oil lamp on the table. "Mamma sent me with these here biscuits for yore supper. She said Miss 'Vanna cookin' ham."

Wiping her hands on a towel, Savannah laughed and stepped forward. "Mamie knows how much I like her biscuits. She's a dear for sending these." She took the pan and set it on the table. "Don't leave, Abraham. I have something for all of you, too. Some of my fried peach pies."

Abraham's eyes lit up. "Fried peach pies? I reckon we ain't had none of them in a long time."

Dante chuckled. "Savannah and her aunt dried these peaches last year, but I imagine we'll all be having peach pies next summer. Savannah told me that we have to get the orchards cleaned up and the trees pruned. Maybe there'll be a bumper crop of apples and peaches to dry."

Abraham nodded. "That sounds good to me, Mistuh Dante. We's gwine make Cottonwood like it used to be."

Savannah handed him the pies and smiled. "Yes we are, Abraham. Maybe even better. Dante tells me that we may soon have another person living with us. A young woman named Hattie. Is that right?"

Abraham backed toward the door, a grin on his face. "Yas'm, I 'spects it won't be long now."

Savannah reached around him and opened the door. "I'm glad. We'll look forward to seeing her."

Dante studied Savannah as she closed the door behind Abraham and walked back to the stove. She hummed a tune under her breath. A sheen of perspiration covered her brow from standing over the hot stove, but Dante thought he'd never seen anyone more beautiful in his life.

Two hours later, with the meal finished and the dishes washed, Savannah sat in her rocking chair mending a pair of socks. Dante glanced up from the passage he'd just read in the Bible and let his gaze drift around the cabin once more. This wasn't where he'd wanted to bring Savannah, but tonight, for some reason, he felt happy just to be here with his wife. He'd never known as much contentment as she'd brought into his life in the last few months.

She glanced up from her sewing and smiled. Laying the socks aside, she rose and picked up Aunt Jane's oil lamp from the table beside her. "It's been a long day. I think I'll go to bed."

He closed his Bible and stood. "Let me get the quilts for my pallet before you go in the bedroom."

Savannah's fingers grasped his arm. "No, Dante. There's no need for that."

He turned to her, a frown on his face. "What do you mean?"

She took a deep breath. "I think it's time you stopped sleeping on the floor. There's no need for that when we have a perfectly good bed."

His eyes grew wide, and he swallowed. "Do you understand what you're saying, Savannah?"

She nodded. "You told me to let you know when I wanted you to be my husband in every sense of the word, and that time has come."

He reached out and trailed his fingers down Savannah's cheek. "You're so beautiful, Savannah, and I want to be your husband. First, though, I must be honest with you and tell you that I have loved you since the day you almost ran me down with that buggy. I know I can't expect you to love me, so you may wish to take back what you've just said. I never want you to feel pressured by me."

Tears filled her eyes, and she pulled his hand to her mouth and kissed his palm. Her long eyelashes fluttered as she gazed into his face. "But I do love you, Dante. I have for a long time. All I want is to be with you for the rest of my life."

His arms circled her and pulled her against him. "That's all I want, too."

She stretched on her tiptoes toward him, and their lips met in the kiss that sealed their marriage vows.

❧

Savannah stared out the window as the first rays of morning light spread across the yard. Lucifer, her favorite rooster, crowed from the henhouse, and it sent a thrill through her. She'd always loved that early morning sound.

Walking to the stove, she picked up the coffeepot and filled Dante's cup. She set the pot back on the stove and caressed Dante's shoulder before she sat down at the kitchen table. The beginning of a new day always excited her, but today it was more. They were beginning a new life together. His eyes sparkled as he gazed at her and talked about what he'd planned for the morning.

"We've cleared the land and marked off the spot for Saul and Mamie's house. I'm going into Willow Bend to order the first building supplies. Do you want to come along?"

Savannah took a sip of her coffee and thought about his invitation. "I'd like that. Maybe I could go by Sarah Morgan's house and visit with her while you're getting what you need. She hasn't been in church for the past few weeks. Her son Seth has been sick."

Dante pushed up from the table. "I like Sarah. She's treated me better than anybody else in Willow Bend."

"She's a good friend of mine and would never do anything to hurt me."

He regarded her with a playful stare. "Are you saying that the way the good people around here treat me is painful to you?"

She made a face at him, stood, and began to stack their

dishes. "Of course. I want everyone to know you and like you as I do."

She turned to place the dishes in the dry sink, but he caught her by the arm. "You said last night you love me. Do you really?"

She laughed and swatted at his arm. "How many times are you going to make me say it?"

His grip tightened. "Savannah, I still can't believe. . ." He stopped at the sound of horses galloping to a stop in front of their cabin.

"Hello in the house!"

Dante released her, walked to the window, and peered out. "It's Sheriff Newton and several men."

Savannah grabbed her shawl and followed Dante to the front porch. Stopping behind him, she stared at the men who faced them and flinched inwardly at the ragtag bunch who rode with the sheriff. She'd known most of them all her life, and they were nothing but drunkards and troublemakers. Just the type of men she'd expect their sheriff to have as friends.

"Good morning, Sheriff Newton," Dante said. "Kind of early to come visiting, isn't it?"

The sheriff spit a wad of tobacco to the ground, wiped his hand across his handlebar mustache, and pushed his hat up on his head. "This ain't no social visit. I just need to know where you were last night."

"I was right here with my wife."

The sheriff's gaze drifted to Savannah. "That right, Miss Carmichael? Was he here?"

Savannah stepped closer to Dante. "Yes, Sheriff, he was. And my name is Mrs. Rinaldi."

He glanced over at one of the men, who snickered, and then looked back to her. "Oh yeah, that's right. You did marry this carpetbagger, didn't you?"

Savannah could feel Dante tense, and she touched his arm. "State your business here, please."

The man leaned forward and rested his arm on the saddle. "Somebody rode through that Crossroads shantytown last night and shot it up right good. Probably the work of outsiders. So that's what made me think of Mr. Rinaldi first."

Dante took a step forward. "Was anybody hurt?"

"Some killed. A few hurt. No great loss. They're just a bunch of ex-slaves."

"Ex-slaves?" Savannah gasped. "You're the law, and you're supposed to be protecting everyone." She crossed her arms and glared at him. "But then I remember how you treated all the freed slaves after the war. You're a disgrace to your office."

The sheriff's face turned crimson, and he pointed a finger at Savannah. "Now just a minute."

Dante held up a hand. "You've gotten the answer to your question about my whereabouts last night. Now I suggest you ride on and look for whoever did this horrible deed."

The sheriff glared at the couple for a moment before he whirled his horse and nodded to the men. "Let's get out of here. I smell a yellow-bellied abolitionist."

Savannah and Dante watched as they rode away. When they'd disappeared, Savannah turned to Dante. Tears filled her eyes. "Oh Dante, some of Cottonwood's people are still living there. We need to find out what happened."

He reached for her hand and guided her back inside. "I'll get Henry Walton to ride over there with me. I think it might be safer for the other men to stay here today. I'll come back as soon as I know anything."

He grabbed his coat from the peg by the door and rushed out. Savannah sank down in the kitchen chair and buried her face in her hands. The sheriff's words rang in her mind, but she knew that he spoke only what so many people in the area thought. The war had left some wounds that it might take years to heal. She wondered if it would happen in her lifetime.

eleven

The Crossroads settlement looked nothing like Dante remembered from the day he'd escorted the families from there to Cottonwood. No children played along the dirt paths that snaked between the shacks, and he couldn't see any groups of young people. Instead, deadly silence covered the area.

Dante reined his horse to a stop and climbed down. He stood in the middle of the road and looked around in disbelief. Wisps of smoke curled upward from the remains of several hovels along the edge of the settlement. He counted five others that, although they still stood, had sustained damage from fire.

Henry dismounted and glanced around. "It looks deserted. Where is everybody?"

Dante shook his head. "I don't know."

Henry held the reins of his horse out to Dante. "I'll see if I can find anybody."

"I'll come with you."

"I think you'd better stay here. I 'spect most white men ain't welcome 'round here today. I lived with them, so I think they'll talk to me."

Dante took the reins of Henry's horse. "All right."

Henry nodded and disappeared along the path that led inside the community. A cold wind blew from the river at the edge of the settlement and whipped about Dante's legs. He looked at the makeshift homes the people lived in and wondered how they kept warm.

The residents of Cottonwood might be living in former slave quarters, but he had made sure that each family had what they needed to keep warm this winter. He doubted if the people at the Crossroads were similarly equipped, and now some of them had lost what little they did have.

The longer Henry stayed gone, the colder Dante became. He tied the horses to a tree beside the road and paced up and down in an attempt to keep warm. Crossing his arms, he hugged himself and wished he could be with Savannah in their warm cabin.

As always, thoughts of her made his heart pump faster. She'd said she loved him, but did she? Was she mistaking her grateful feelings to be back at Cottonwood for love? Doubt drifted into his mind. He wanted to believe her, but uncertainty remained. Even though he'd been thrilled to hear her words, he had to be careful. The community still considered him an outsider, and Savannah might very well harbor some of those same feelings. Only time would tell.

Dante glanced at the deserted settlement again and wondered where everyone had gone. He began pacing again, lost in thought. After what seemed an eternity, Henry reappeared. A sad look lined his face.

Dante met him at the end of the path. "Did you find anybody?"

Henry nodded. "Yes. They're all in a field back of here, burying the dead."

"Do they need help?"

"Yeah, they do, but they're mighty upset right now. Don't hardly want to see nobody."

Dante took a deep breath. "How many died?"

Henry's forehead wrinkled, and his chin quivered. "Ten.

Two entire families that lived in those huts that burned to the ground."

Dante shook his head in disbelief. "But how did this happen?"

"They said a rebel yell woke them up in the middle of the night. Six men on horses were outside. They had on hoods and held torches. They set fire to some of the houses, and when the people ran out, they shot 'em down."

Dante choked back the nausea rolling in his stomach. "Women and children, too?"

"Yes." Henry wiped at his eyes and blinked. "The folks scattered, but the riders came after them, yelling and shooting. When the men finished havin' their fun, they rode off."

Dante put his hand on Henry's shoulder. "Did you know the ones who were killed?"

Henry blinked back tears and stared at Dante. "Abraham's Hattie, her father, mother, and brother are all dead. How we gonna tell Abraham?"

Dante shook his head. "I don't know." He remembered how happy Abraham had looked the night before when he told Savannah about the young woman he wanted to marry. "You said the men wore hoods?"

"Yes."

"Did anyone see anything familiar about them?"

"They know who done it."

Dante frowned. "But the sheriff came by home this morning, and he didn't know who they were. Why haven't they told him?"

Henry grunted in disgust. " 'Cause they know he won't do nothing to the owner of Oak Hill Plantation."

Dante's mouth gaped in surprise. "Jonathan Boyer? How do they know?"

"Some of the men are former slaves from Oak Hill. They recognized his horse. He was the leader of the bunch."

Dante rubbed his hand over his eyes. "Oh, this is going to be rough on Savannah. Jonathan has been her friend all her life."

"Well, they say he's a right mean man, and they don't want to do nothing else to make him mad." Henry glanced back the way he had come out of the settlement. "They're havin' a hard time diggin' them graves. They only got one shovel. Folks are just scratching at the ground with whatever they got."

Dante took a deep breath. "We need to help. It'll take too long to go to Cottonwood for shovels. I'll go into town and get some at the store. You go on back and tell them. I'll return as soon as I can."

Henry nodded. "Yes, sir. I reckon they'll be much obliged."

Dante untied the reins of his horse and swung into the saddle. "I'll be back as soon as I can."

He dug his heels into the horse's sides and leaned forward as the horse galloped away. He'd known Jonathan Boyer was filled with anger, but he never would have suspected him of murder.

Then there was Abraham. He had no idea how he was going to break this horrible news to him. As he rode toward town, he prayed for the survivors of last night's raid. The people at the Crossroads had suffered for years as slaves. Freedom had only brought them different problems. As free men and women, they hadn't been able to escape the cruelty of men determined to make them suffer.

Men like Jonathan Boyer couldn't believe the changes the war had brought to the South. Instead of accepting the way life was now, they chose to harbor anger that festered like giant sores in their souls. And who better to unleash their anger on than the people they perceived as the ones who caused their way of life to collapse.

Until the ones who raided the Crossroads were caught, no former slaves in the county would be safe. Someone had to put a stop to Jonathan Boyer and his band of murderers.

❧

Savannah put her sewing aside, got up from her chair, and walked to the window. Dante still hadn't come home, and the sun had already begun to dip behind the horizon. She peered outside, but he and Henry were nowhere in sight.

Ever since he left earlier in the day, she had tried to keep busy, but she couldn't get her mind off what the sheriff had said. If some of the people were hurt, she and Mamie could be of help. But if they were needed, Dante would have sent for her.

She sighed and trudged to the stove to check the beans that simmered in the pot. She stirred them and thought of Aunt Jane's insistence on their having a vegetable garden last summer. Thank goodness for the bounty they'd had. It had come in handy to feed all the mouths that now lived at Cottonwood.

She replaced the lid on the pot and turned back to her chair just as the door opened and Dante walked in. Patches of dirt smudged his face and coat, but it was the look on his face that sent shivers through her.

Her throat went dry, and she tried to swallow. "How bad was it?"

He pulled off his gloves and rubbed his hand across his face. "Ten dead. Henry and I helped dig the graves."

Her hand went to her throat, and her heart pounded. "Were any of them Cottonwood people?"

He shook his head. "I don't think so. It seems that the Oak

Hill former slaves suffered more than any."

She hurried across the room and stood in front of him. "Oh no. I knew some of them. How awful this must be for Jonathan."

His face darkened, and his body shook with anger. "Awful? I doubt it since he and his friends were the ones who did it."

She'd never seen Dante so upset, and it scared her. Shaking her head, she reached for his coat. "Let me help you with your coat. I know you're upset, but it's ridiculous to blame Jonathan for something like this."

He pulled away from her. "And why would you think that?"

"Because I know him, and he's not a murderer."

He regarded her with a steady gaze. "Have you forgotten how he's behaved ever since we married? You said the war changed him, and I think it made him into some kind of monster."

Her cheeks burned, but she stared back at him. "He lost his way of life in the war, and he's just rebelling against that. But Jonathan would never commit murder."

Fists clenched at his sides, he advanced on her. "How can you defend him?"

She trembled at his anger. "B–because I've known him all my life. He couldn't kill anyone."

"Well, he did!" Dante shouted.

She took another step back. "Did anybody see him?"

"No, they wore hoods."

"Then how did they know it was Jonathan?"

He leaned toward her. "Some of them recognized his horse."

"His horse? Lots of horses look alike. It could have been anybody with a horse that looked like his."

Dante advanced on her, and she backed away until she felt

the kitchen table behind her. He stopped in front of her and stared at her for a moment. "So you're choosing to stand up for a killer."

Tears spilled from her eyes. "Please understand, Dante."

His body sagged, and he backed away. "I do. He's an old friend, and I'm an outsider who happened to trap you into marriage. I thought you were different from everybody else in Willow Bend, but you're not. Instead of believing your husband, who talked to the people Boyer attacked, you choose to defend him." He took a deep breath and turned toward the door. "I have to go see Abraham and tell him the news."

Stunned by Dante's last words, Savannah rushed forward and stopped him. "What do you have to tell Abraham?"

He regarded her with an icy glare. "That Hattie was one of the people Jonathan gunned down last night. I dug her grave myself."

She pressed her hand to her mouth. "No, please tell me that's not true."

He took a deep breath. "Oh, but it is. I buried her right next to her parents and her brother while Henry was digging the grave of a woman and her baby."

Tears streamed down her face, and she reached out to Dante. "You're upset over what you've seen today. What can I do to help you?"

He stared at her hand before he pulled away from her grasp. "There's nothing you can do. I don't understand people who hate that much, and I don't understand those that close their eyes to the evil around them." He took a deep breath. "I should never have come to Willow Bend. I'll always be an outsider here."

Before Savannah could respond, he walked out of the cabin. She stared at the closed door a moment before she bent forward and pressed her forehead to the cool wood.

Her heart thudded at the memory of Dante's face and the words he'd said. He sounded as if he thought she'd chosen between him and Jonathan. That wasn't true. She only needed to make some sense out of the whole situation.

Her words hurt Dante. He didn't mean it when he said he never should have come to Willow Bend. If he hadn't come, she never would have met him, and they wouldn't be married. And if they hadn't married, she might never have fallen in love.

Her eyes widened, and she covered her mouth with her hand. The way Dante had spoken sounded as if he didn't believe she really loved him. If that was the case, she had to find a way to show him that he was the most important thing in her life. The loss of Cottonwood was nothing compared to what it would be like to lose Dante.

ತಿ

Dante stopped on the porch of the cabin and pondered what he should do. He hadn't meant to speak so sharply to Savannah, but her words had ripped his heart. Ever since they'd been married, he'd done everything he could to make her trust him. Just last night she'd said she loved him, yet she still chose Jonathan over him.

He'd spoken in anger, and that wasn't like him at all. He never should have said what he did about not coming to Willow Bend. The best things that had ever happened in his life had occurred here. He'd always dreamed of owning land, and now he did, but he wanted more. He wanted his wife's love.

He raked his hand through his hair. Maybe what he'd feared all along was true. Savannah had married him so she could come back to Cottonwood, and she had played the part of his wife well. But that's all it was—just a role like in a play so that she could keep her end of the bargain.

Dante shook the thoughts from his head. Other things needed to be faced now.

He glanced at the cabin a short distance away and knew that Saul's family waited inside for news of friends. With a heavy heart, he stepped off the porch and headed toward their cabin.

Before he could knock on the door, it flew open. Saul stood in the lamplight from inside. A worried expression lined his face. "Mistuh Dante, we's been worried 'bout you and Henry. What you find out?"

Dante looked past Saul to Mamie, Abraham, and Joshua, who hovered in the room behind. He didn't have the words to tell Abraham what he had come to say. That news needed to come from his father.

He cleared his throat and motioned for Saul to follow him outside. When they stood alone on the porch, Dante related the events of the day. As he told of burying Hattie's body, tears burned his eyes, and he wiped at them.

Saul stood speechless, his mouth slightly open. When Dante finished, he put his hand on Saul's shoulder. "I thought it best if this news came from you. You'll know how to tell Abraham."

Saul's lips quivered, and he gazed past Dante toward the remains of the big house. "When we heared the war was over and we was free, we thought life was gwine be good for us, but that ain't the way it's been."

"I know," Dante murmured. "It may take a long time for things to change in the South, but it will, Saul. Someday it will be different."

"Someday ain't gwine help those what died at the Crossroads.

All they wanted was to live like ev'rybody else what's free." He paused as if he was remembering the past. After a moment he exhaled. "Bein' owned by somebody is a hard life. My mamma is jest a little picture in my mind 'cause I got sold off when I was 'bout the age of Big Mike's youngest. Don't know nothin' 'bout my pappy."

Pain radiated through the words. Dante thought of his own mother and father and how he would have felt as a boy to be separated from them. "But your life was good at Cottonwood, wasn't it?"

Saul nodded. "Might say that. Leastways, none of mine ever got sold, but others did. When we first heared that Mr. Lincoln wanted to free us, we all talked 'bout where we'd go and what we'd do. Oh, we made big plans, but they warn't no use. Cain't go nowhere without money, and we didn't have none. Just had each other. Now Abraham gwine find out he ain't got what he wanted."

Dante searched for some words of comfort, but nothing came to mind. "Saul, I know how you must feel, but we'll get through this."

Saul stared at him with tortured eyes. He took a deep breath. "You a good man, Mistuh Dante, but I 'spects you cain't know how I feels. Only a man what's been owned by somebody can understand."

Saul turned and walked back into his home. "God," Dante whispered, "watch over this family. Comfort them during this awful time."

A shout from the cabin jerked Dante's attention back to the people inside.

"No! No! No!" Abraham's voice cried out.

Dante stepped off the porch and stared at the soft light coming from his cabin. Inside, Savannah waited. He didn't want to see her right now, and she probably didn't want to see him either. It would be better for them to be apart for a while.

Without glancing at the cabin again, he strode toward the barn. He needed time to think.

twelve

Savannah sat at the kitchen table, holding a book she'd brought from Aunt Jane's, but she couldn't keep her mind on the words. Dante had left two hours ago to tell Abraham about Hattie, but he hadn't returned. Loneliness washed over her, and she wished he would come back.

She glanced around the cabin where she'd lived for the last four months. With Aunt Jane's familiar belongings scattered about, it had begun to feel like home—hers and Dante's.

She touched the surface of the oak table that had once belonged to her grandmother and remembered the times she and Aunt Jane had shared together there. Across the room, the elegant sideboard Aunt Jane's husband had given her before the war stood against the wall. Most of the other furnishings from the Willow Bend house were stored in an empty cabin, but she'd insisted they find room for these. They held many memories for her.

With a sigh, she closed the book and stood. Pulling her shawl from around her shoulders, she hung it on the back of the chair and checked Dante's supper on the back of the stove.

The squirrel stew still simmered in the pot, but it was going to be ruined if he didn't come soon. The memory of his sad face flickered in her mind, and she shivered. She hadn't meant to hurt him. If he would only come back, she would apologize.

A noise from the front porch caught her attention, and she

turned. Dante entered the cabin. Relief flowed through her, but she restrained herself from throwing her arms around him. Instead, she clutched at her apron and gathered the material into puckered balls in her hands.

She tried to smile. "I was concerned about you. Where have you been?"

He took off his coat and hung it on the peg. "After I told Saul about Hattie, I went out to the barn. I had a lot of thinking to do."

Her heart pounded, and she struggled to remain calm. "About what?"

"About the war and how it's destroyed so many lives."

She took a step toward him. "We can't do anything about that."

He strode toward her and stopped within inches. His clutched fists dangled at his sides. "But I want to do something. I want to help the people we've brought to Cottonwood, and I grieve for all those who are left drifting without anything— like all those people at Crossroads. They have families, and they just want to be happy. Why can't they?"

She put her hand on his arm. "I don't know, Dante. Attitudes in the South may not change in our lifetime. All we can do is try to make a difference where we are." She stared up into his face, and her heart longed to bring some comfort to him. "You're a good man. You've brought life back to Cottonwood. It's not what it was, but if we work together, we can make it better than before."

The muscle in his jaw twitched. "Do you mean that?"

"Yes."

"You still want to do that?"

She frowned. "Of course I do. Did you think I'd changed my mind?"

"I thought you might regret telling me you loved me."

"Why would you think that?"

"Because of the way I spoke to you earlier. Do you hate me, Savannah?" His dark eyes burned like coals.

She shook her head. "I don't hate you."

His eyes softened, and his gaze traveled over her face. "I'm sorry for what I said. I understand how you feel about Jonathan. He's been your friend for years. I've never had a friend like that. I envy you."

She smiled. "Don't envy my friendship with Jonathan. I've thought about what you said, and I'm sure you're right. The old Jonathan never would have killed anybody, but the man now living at Oak Hill very well could."

He inched closer. "Maybe *envy* isn't the right word. Maybe I'm jealous of him because I love you so much."

She tilted her head and studied his face. Reaching up, she cupped his cheek with her hand. "I love you, too."

His eyes widened. "Are you sorry about that?"

She stroked his face again and shook her head. "No, why would you think that?"

He reached up, took hold of her hand, and brought it to his mouth. His warm lips grazed the palm of her hand. "Because you're so young and beautiful, and I'm ten years older than you. I'm an Italian and an outsider here. I'm different from all the people you've known all your life."

Her stomach fluttered at his whispered words. "Yes, you are, and I thank God for that."

His Adam's apple bobbed. "Maybe. . ."

They jumped in alarm at the sound of someone pounding on the door.

"Mistuh Dante! Mistuh Dante! You in there?"

Dante whirled and ran to the door with Savannah right

behind. She stared over his shoulder at Saul, who stood on the front porch.

"Saul, what's the matter?" Dante demanded.

Tears flowed down Saul's face. "Abraham done went crazy, Mistuh Dante. He kept saying he gwine take him a horse and go find those men what killed Hattie. I tole him he be a thief if'n he took yo' horse, but he did it. He done took my squirrel rifle and gone. What we gwine do, Mistuh Dante?"

Dante pulled the shaking man into the house and closed the door. "Calm down, Saul. You say Abraham took a horse and went after the men who killed Hattie?"

"Yas suh, but he ain't a thief, Mistuh Dante. Doan be mad at him."

Dante reached for his coat. "It's all right, Saul. I know Abraham isn't a thief. He's just upset. Maybe we can catch him."

He turned to Savannah. "Saul and I will go after Abraham. I don't know when we'll be back."

"B–but where will you look?"

Dante's eyes narrowed in thought. "We'll go to the Crossroads first. Perhaps he went there to find out who they thought were responsible for the raid."

"Abraham knows who done it, Mistuh Dante."

Saul's low voice sent shivers down Savannah's back. "How does he know?"

"He say when he went to town with Henry last week, he was waitin' by the wagon for Henry to come out of da store. Mistuh Boyer from Oak Hill walked up and tole him to git in the wagon; folks like him warn't 'posed to stand in the way of white folks walkin' down the street. Abraham tole him he warn't blockin' anybody's path, and Mistuh Boyer got right mad. He tole Abraham he'd be sorry he back talked a white man."

Fear rose in Savannah's throat. "Do you think he might go to Oak Hill?"

Dante shook his head. "I don't know." He walked to the sideboard, opened a drawer, and pulled out his pistol. He stared at it for a moment before he tucked it in the waistband of his pants. "We'd better find him before he gets in bad trouble."

The sight of the gun terrified Savannah. In the months of their marriage, she'd never seen Dante even look at it. Now he acted like a man who wouldn't hesitate to use it. He walked back and stopped beside her. She glanced down at the revolver. "Dante, why the gun?"

He straightened his shoulders and buttoned his coat. "In case we run into any trouble."

She grabbed Dante's hands "Then hurry and catch him before that happens. I'll go stay with Mamie and Joshua until you get back. And please be careful."

He glanced down at their intertwined hands and squeezed hers. "We'll try." He released her and turned to Saul. "I'll go to the barn and start saddling the horses. You tell Big Mike and the others where we're going. Tell them to keep an eye on everything until we get back."

Saul nodded and dashed out the door.

Dante hurried onto the front porch. Savannah followed and watched him run to the barn. When he disappeared from sight, she stepped back inside, checked the fire in the stove, and grabbed her shawl from the back of the chair. She paused at the door and breathed a prayer for the safety of Dante, Saul, and Abraham before she hurried outside and ran toward Mamie and Saul's cabin.

❧

Dante and Saul rode through the dark night toward Oak

Hill. In the months Dante had been at Cottonwood, Savannah had often talked about the Boyer plantation and what a grand place it had been before the war, but he'd never been there. Now he raced in its direction on a mission of life and death.

He didn't want to think about what would happen to Abraham if Jonathan and his friends found him first. Even with a squirrel rifle for protection, a young man would be defenseless against a band of angry killers.

Dante glanced at Saul, but in the dark he couldn't make out the expression on the man's face. He must be worried out of his mind for the safety of his son. Saul had told Dante he could never understand what he felt, and Dante knew that was true. Someone who had never experienced slavery couldn't start to comprehend what Saul and all the others had endured.

A horse whinnied in the distance, and Dante and Saul reined to a stop. "Did you hear that?"

Saul pointed at the forest to the right of the road. "Yas suh. It sound like it comin' from those woods over yonder."

Dante turned his horse's head in the direction of the sound and nudged him forward into the inky darkness. Leaves on the forest floor rustled as the horses moved slowly forward. Dante strained to hear another sound, but even the night animals were silent.

His horse raised its head and snorted in surprise at a figure standing between the bare trees. Dante squinted and recognized the horse from Cottonwood, but there was no rider.

"Mistuh Dante, that the horse Abraham took."

Dante got off and walked toward the animal. "Easy, boy."

The horse didn't move, and Dante grabbed the reins that

trailed on the ground. The lather on the horse's back told Dante he had been ridden hard. But where was Abraham?

Dante moved to the side of the animal and stopped. His nostrils flared at the smell that he could identify even in the dark. He'd encountered it innumerable times in the field hospitals where he'd worked. Blood.

He ran his hand over the saddle and felt the sticky substance on his fingers. Saul dismounted and stood beside him.

"Mistuh Dante, what is it?"

"We have to find Abraham right away. Something bad has happened."

Dante grasped the reins of his and Abraham's horses and walked forward. The undergrowth in the forest pulled at his boots, but he ignored it and trudged forward with Saul behind. They'd gone about fifty yards when he stopped short.

Saul halted beside him. "What is it?"

Dante frowned. "I thought I heard something."

A breeze rustled the bare branches of the trees. Dante strained to hear whatever the wind had stirred. It came from straight ahead. He inched forward. The sound, like the creaking of a swaying tree branch, grew louder.

Just as he stepped into a small clearing, the clouds parted, and moonlight filtered down through the trees. Dante stopped and gasped. He saw the rope looped over the limb first and let his gaze travel to the noose at the end. Pain like a kick in the stomach ripped through Dante. Abraham, his hands bound behind him, swung from a branch of an oak tree ahead.

"Saul. . ."

A roar of despair from Saul pierced the quiet of the forest. They dropped the reins of their horses and sprinted toward Abraham's body. Together Dante and Saul grabbed Abraham's legs and lifted him as high as they could.

"Saul," Dante yelled, "hold him while I climb up and cut him down."

Saul clamped his arms around his son's legs and heaved his body higher. Dante pulled the knife from his pocket and opened it before he shinnied up the tree. Easing out onto the branch, he sawed at the rope until it gave way and Abraham's body tumbled downward.

Dante swung his legs off the branch, dropped to the ground, and knelt beside Saul. "Is he breathing?"

Saul frantically tugged the rope from around Abraham's neck and pulled his son to his chest. Tears streamed down his face. "He's dead, Mistuh Dante. They done killed my son. Why they have to go and do a thing like that?"

Dante reached out and grasped the man's shaking shoulder. There was no answer to ease Saul's anguish. All Dante could do was sit beside him as he cried out his grief.

thirteen

Savannah stood at the window in Saul and Mamie's cabin and stared into the dark night. Dante and Saul had left hours ago. What if they had encountered Jonathan's men and were lying hurt or even dead on the road to Oak Hill? She gritted her teeth. No, she wouldn't think that way. They'd come riding up anytime now with Abraham in tow.

She glanced over her shoulder at Mamie, who stared into the fireplace's flames. Savannah's heart ached for her. Although Mamie loved her younger son, Joshua, Abraham was her special child, the one who'd always done everything he could to make life easier for his mother.

Savannah's brow wrinkled into a deep frown. Tomorrow she was going to give Abraham a good tongue-lashing. Even though he'd suffered a tragic loss, he should know better than to cause his mother such anguish. After she got through scolding him, he would think before he did it again.

"Where Joshua?" Mamie's voice from behind caught her attention.

"He went to the barn to check on the livestock."

Turning from the window, Savannah walked over to Mamie and put her hand on her shoulder. "Can I fix you something? A cup of coffee? Or maybe something to eat?"

Mamie shook her head. "Don't reckon my stomach would take kindly to nothin' right now, Miss 'Vanna, but I thanks you."

The cabin door opened, and Joshua stepped inside. Savannah gazed at the young man. At eighteen, he was four years younger than his older brother. Savannah had always thought it remarkable that Abraham could be so like Mamie, spirited and fun loving, while Joshua resembled his father in looks and disposition.

Both of Mamie's sons worked hard in the fields during the day, but in other ways they differed. Joshua's serious nature kept him focused on work and family responsibilities, while Abraham loved to sing and tell stories to anyone who would listen. Savannah remembered how the girls in the slave quarters all fell under his spell at one time or another, but he never noticed any of them until Hattie. Savannah wondered how she had been able to capture the wild heart of the young man.

Joshua walked over to his mother and bent over her. "Mamma, I done checked the livestock. I reckon they be all right till morning. Now I thinks I'll jest wait in the other room till Abraham gets home. You need me to do anything else for you?"

Mamie shook her head. "I'm fine. Me and Miss 'Vanna gwine wait right here till they gets back."

Joshua bent and kissed his mother on the cheek. "You calls out if'n you need me."

"I will." Mamie turned her head and watched Joshua enter the small room that served as a bedroom for him and Abraham. When he closed the door, she smiled at Savannah. "Joshua, he a good son. He goin' in there to pray for his brother."

"He and Abraham both are good sons." Savannah knelt beside the woman she'd loved all her life. "Mamie, Dante and Saul will find Abraham and bring him home. We just have to believe that."

Mamie clutched her hands in her lap. "My head tells me that, but it my heart that don't believe it. I feels like my whole insides just torn to pieces."

Savannah covered Mamie's hands with hers. "I can understand how you feel."

Mamie's lips quivered. "He my firstborn. He real special 'cause I had a hard time birthin' him. I don't knows how I can live if'n somethin' done happened to him."

Savannah gasped. "Don't say that. Don't even think that."

Sadness lined Mamie's face. "You don't knows how I feel, but you will when your baby born."

Savannah chuckled. "Don't rush things, Mamie. That won't happen for a long time."

"Don't wait too long, Miss 'Vanna."

Savannah opened her mouth to speak, but the sound of a horse's whinny from outside stopped her. She grasped Mamie's hands. "They're back."

Fear flickered in Mamie's eyes. "You go see, Miss 'Vanna. I don't thinks my feet gwine move."

Savannah nodded and grabbed the oil lamp sitting on the kitchen table. Without waiting to grab her shawl, she ran to the door and bolted onto the porch. She held the lamp high. The small beam flickered across the yard, and Dante's horse moved into its small circle of light. Relief poured through her at the sight of her husband.

She rushed down the steps and hurried to stand beside his horse. He climbed down, but his silence scared her. "Did you find him?"

"Yes." The word, spoken so softly, was almost a whisper.

She glanced over his shoulder and caught sight of Saul, but she didn't see Abraham. "Then where is he?"

In the dim light she could see his face, and she gasped. She'd seen suffering before, but she'd never encountered anything as horrible as the tortured look on Dante's face.

His lips quivered, and he tried to speak. She looked from

him to Saul, who had dismounted. She stepped around Dante and held the lamp up higher. Her eyes widened at the sight of the third horse, a body across the saddle. Her hand shook, and the lamp dipped toward the ground.

Saul stepped forward. "They kilt Abraham, Miss 'Vanna. Them men hung him from a tree and kilt my son."

"My baby." The scream pierced the air, and Savannah turned to see Mamie running toward Saul. "I wants to see my baby."

Saul dropped the reins to his horse and grabbed her. Her eyes had the look of a wild woman, and she beat at Saul with her fists. Saul let her fight at him until her cries turned to whimpers and her hands rested against his chest. Then he wrapped his arms around her and cradled her like a suffering child. "It gwine be all right, Mamie. I here with you."

The doors of the other cabins opened, and the tenant farmers of Cottonwood and their families slipped from their homes to join the mourning family. Savannah glanced back at the porch. Joshua stared at the horse carrying his brother's body. He drifted down the steps and stopped next to his parents.

No one spoke. Savannah looked around the group of mourners. She hadn't seen such sorrow since the night of her parents' deaths. Tears streamed down her face, and she looked up at Dante. "Why would Jonathan do this?"

"I don't know."

Saul reached out to Joshua and drew him into the circle of his arms. Savannah hoped Saul's touch offered some measure of comfort to Mamie and Joshua.

She looked up at Dante and wanted to feel that from him. She stepped closer to him and laid her head on his chest. His arms encircled her and drew her closer. She buried her face in his chest and cried for the war that had destroyed so many lives, for her parents, for Abraham, and for the people whose freedom had only brought them new problems.

***

Dante entered the cabin, hung up his coat, and opened the drawer of the sideboard. He pulled the gun from his pants waistband and laid it inside. On the ride home, he'd asked himself many times if he could have used it if he'd gotten there before they hung Abraham.

Thou shalt not kill.

The words echoed in his mind, but he knew he could have pulled the trigger to save Abraham's life. He clenched his fists and banged them against the wall. It didn't matter now what he could have done. Abraham was dead.

He slammed the drawer closed and strode to the stove. Opening the firebox, he shoved another piece of wood inside and adjusted the dampers to increase the blaze. He closed the door and held his hands over the stovetop. They still burned from the icy cold of the night.

His thoughts went to Savannah and how she had cried when they brought Abraham's body back earlier. Although his heart ached, too, it felt good to have her in his arms.

He sighed and wondered if Pinky and Big Mike had finished the coffin. He'd stayed with them in the barn until they were almost finished, but he'd been unable to help much. Pinky possessed the best carpentry skills at Cottonwood, and he'd been quick to set to work on the task.

Dante walked to the window and looked out. Savannah and the other women must still be at Saul and Mamie's. None of the men or their wives had looked surprised when Savannah took over the arrangements for Abraham's body. Before he knew it, there had been a cover placed on Mamie's kitchen table, and Savannah had supervised the moving of Abraham's body there. Then she'd sent Mamie and Saul home with Henry and Mary Ann Walton while she, Tildy, and Big Mike's wife, Josie, prepared Abraham for burial. He wondered how long it would take.

He sat down at the kitchen table and pulled the piece of paper out of his pocket that Saul had found inside Abraham's shirt. With no light in the dark woods, he hadn't been able to make out the words. Now he unfolded it and spread it out in front of him.

The printed words that spilled across the paper sent an icy chill through his body. His hands shook, and he pulled the paper closer to make sure he read it correctly: *Cottonwood Is Next.*

Abraham's killers had sent a message to him. Dante jumped up from his chair, and it toppled over backward and clattered to the floor. What could he do? Telling the sheriff wouldn't help. For all he knew, the sheriff was as guilty as Jonathan Boyer.

He scooped the note up and stuck it in his pocket. Savannah didn't need to know about this. He would decide how he and the Cottonwood residents could best protect their homes and families before he alarmed her.

The door opened, and Savannah entered the cabin. The red spots dotting her cheeks had to be caused by the cold night air, but the redness of her eyes told him she'd been crying. She set the lamp she carried on the table and sank down in a chair. He eased into the one across from her.

"How are Mamie and Saul?"

Savannah rubbed her eyes and shook her head. "They're in shock. They can't believe this has happened."

"Did you complete the burial preparations?"

Savannah took a deep breath. "Yes. Pinky and Big Mike brought the coffin just as we got through. Big Mike and Joshua placed Abraham's body in it. I went over to Mary Ann's and brought Mamie and Saul home. Mamie nearly collapsed when she saw Abraham. Tildy and Josie are going to stay with them until morning. They don't need to be alone."

"I can understand."

Savannah glanced up at him, and fresh tears ran down her face. "How are they ever going to live with this? Their son has been murdered for no reason." Her eyes hardened, and she gritted her teeth. "And knowing our good sheriff as I do, he'll find every excuse he can to put off looking for the killers. If he looked very hard, he might find them, and he doesn't want to do that."

Dante wanted to take her in his arms and tell her that everything was going to be all right, but the note in his pocket reminded him there still might be battles ahead. The thought that he might lose Savannah as Abraham had lost Hattie and as Saul and Mamie had lost their son terrified him. He had to protect her at all costs.

Dante leaned back in his chair. "You're tired and upset. Why don't you go on to bed? You'll feel better in the morning."

She wiped at her eyes and nodded. "That's a good idea. You're tired, too. Maybe a good night's sleep will help us both." She rose from the table and walked toward the bedroom. At the door she stopped. "Aren't you coming to bed?"

"No. I think I'll enjoy the warmth of the stove for a while. You go on."

She hesitated a moment. "All right. Good night."

"Good night, Savannah."

She closed the door, but he waited until he saw the lamplight underneath the door disappear and heard the bed creak. Then he pulled the note from his pocket again. Smoothing it out on the tabletop, he reread the message.

He stared at the words for a moment before he sighed and stood up. Crossing the room, he drew the gun from the sideboard drawer and pulled his rifle down from where it hung on the wall. He sat at the table and laid the guns on top next to the note. If they had any visitors at Cottonwood tonight, he was going to be ready.

❧

Savannah awoke, her body shaking from the cold. Even though darkness covered the room, she knew Dante had not come to bed. She had no idea how long she'd slept, but she supposed it must be the middle of the night.

She slipped from underneath the covers and reached for the shawl on the chair beside the bed. Her feet touched the cold floor, and her skin prickled at the icy feel. She hurried across the room and opened the door.

The oil lamp still burned on the table. Its glow cast an eerie light across the room and the figure slumped at the table. She eased into the room and stood beside her husband, bent over in sleep. She reached out to wake him, but she spied the note underneath his spread fingers.

She frowned and slipped it free of his grasp. He stirred, and she held her breath. When he settled back into his restless sleep, she picked the paper up and read what was printed on it. Her eyes grew wide at the words, but a greater fear flowed through her at the sight of the weapons on the table.

She didn't know where or when Dante had received the note, but she understood his concern. He'd stayed up to guard their home while she slept, but his tired body had not been up to the task. She slipped the note under his hand and backed away from the table.

Aunt Jane's cedar chest sat against the bedroom wall, and she hurried to it and pulled out a patchwork quilt Aunt Jane had made years ago. She returned to the kitchen, stopped behind Dante's chair, and draped the quilt around his shoulders.

Savannah stared at his handsome face. Even as he slept, she could make out the lines of fatigue caused by his desire to make Cottonwood productive again and to rebuild the lives of the tenant farmers he'd brought there. Guilt pricked at her heart. She, too, contributed to his worries when she had defended Jonathan to him. The responsibilities he'd taken on in the past few months would defeat a lesser man, but not Dante. She'd never known anyone who had the strength of body and of character like he had.

Her heart burst with love for him, and she leaned over and kissed him on the cheek. She pulled her shawl tighter around her, scooted a chair closer to the stove, and sat down. Dante could sleep until morning. She'd keep watch for him.

fourteen

A sound jerked Dante from his deep sleep. His cheek lay against a wooden surface. He blinked to remember where he was. The memory of trying to stay awake to keep watch flashed into his mind. He bolted into a sitting position and turned his head in the direction of whatever had awakened him.

Savannah closed the oven door and set down a pan of biscuits. She wiped her hands on her apron and smiled at him. "I wondered how long you were going to sleep."

His gaze darted across the tabletop, but the note was nowhere to be seen. "H–how long have you been up?"

She kept her attention directed at a skillet on the stove top and didn't look around. "Oh, for some time now. I started to wake you, but I decided not to."

He looked under the table and around the bottom of his chair. The note had disappeared. He straightened and glanced at Savannah. She stood facing him with her arms crossed and a frown on her face. "Did you lose something?"

"Just a piece of paper. I'm sure it's around here somewhere." He bent over and looked underneath the table again.

"Is this what you lost?" The note dangled from her fingers.

He slumped back in his chair. "So you've seen it?"

She walked to the table and sat down opposite him. "Where did you get this?"

He rubbed his hands over his eyes. "It was in Abraham's shirt."

Her eyes narrowed and she nodded. "I thought it must

have something to do with the lynching. What were you going to do? Stay up all night, guarding the house?"

He shook his head. "I don't know what I was thinking. I just knew I had to keep watch." He gave a disgusted grunt. "Some sentry I am. I couldn't even stay awake. What if they'd come while I was asleep?"

She smiled. "Oh, I don't know. Maybe I would have heard them since I took over after I found you asleep."

His mouth gaped open in surprise. "You stayed up after I went to sleep?"

She laughed and stood up. "I thought one of us ought to be alert, and you were sleeping so soundly I didn't have the heart to wake you."

"I'm sorry you missed your sleep."

"No need for that." He watched as she went back to the stove and picked up the coffeepot. She poured two cups and scooted one toward him. "Drink this. It'll help you awaken so that we can talk about what we're going to do."

"We?"

She bent over him, her face only a few inches from his. "If I remember correctly, you told me when we married that this land is mine, too. And I don't intend to let anyone harm it or any of its people. Do you understand?"

His heart hammered in his chest as he stared into her eyes. "Yes, I understand. If I didn't know better, I'd think I married a woman determined to have a henpecked husband."

She blushed and turned away. "I don't think you would ever let anybody make you do anything you didn't want to."

He stared at her as she set the coffeepot on the stove. There was something different about Savannah. In the last few days, she'd acted happier than he'd ever seen her. It thrilled him to think her feelings for him might have something to do with that. He sat up straighter and noticed for the first time the quilt draped around his shoulders.

He rubbed his fingers over the cover. "Where did this come from?"

She turned, the pan of biscuits in one hand and a plate of eggs in the other, and set them in front of him. "I put it there. I didn't want you to get cold."

Her face glowed, and he wondered if it was from the heat of the stove. "Thank you."

She sat in the chair across from him, picked up her coffee, and took a sip. He set his cup down and stared into its depth. "Last night seems like a bad dream."

"I know. I keep thinking of how Mamie and Saul looked when they saw Abraham in the coffin." She closed her eyes for a moment, frowned, and shook her head. When she opened her eyes, she blinked back tears. "I need to go over there so Tildy and Josie can go feed their families."

He swallowed a bite of eggs and pointed to her coffee cup with his fork. "Aren't you eating anything this morning?"

She picked up her cup and took a sip. "I ate a biscuit before you woke up."

"You need to eat something else. It's going to be a long day."

"I know." She set the cup down. "What do you have planned for this morning?"

He took a deep breath. "I'm going to see the sheriff first thing and tell him what's happened. I doubt if he'll do anything about it. Then I'm going to the store and buy some extra rifles and ammunition."

"Do you think they'll attack us like they did the people at the Crossroads?"

"I wouldn't doubt it. If they come here, I mean for our people to be ready for them."

"You'll be back in time for the burial, won't you?"

"I will."

"Then eat your breakfast and go to town. We'll be ready when you get back." She pushed up from the table and walked to the door. Her shawl hung on a peg beside it, and she reached for it. She pulled the wrap around her and opened the door. Before she stepped into the cold morning, she turned and smiled. "Be careful, Dante."

Her quiet words set his heart to pumping. Before he could respond, she walked outside. He restrained himself from rushing after her and sweeping her into his arms. Other matters needed his attention. He had to do everything in his power to see that Savannah and the people of Cottonwood were protected.

❧

Savannah stared at her reflection in the mirror of the walnut dresser that had graced her bedroom at Aunt Jane's and now sat crammed into the tiny room she shared with Dante. Her mind wandering, she pulled the silver-handled brush through her hair. Where could Dante be? He'd been gone since early morning, and now it was well past noon.

She laid the brush down and stood to smooth the wrinkles from her dress. As she ran her palms down the length of the skirt, she remembered the last time she'd worn this dress— the day she'd married Dante.

Backing up from the dresser, she twisted at the waist to get a better view of herself. She remembered how uncertain about her decision she'd been that day. Now she couldn't understand why she would have ever doubted saying yes to his proposal.

"What are you doing?"

She jumped at the sound of his voice. He stood in the open door, a puzzled expression on his face.

She reached for the brush on the dresser and pulled it through her hair once more. "I just finished dressing for Abraham's burial, and I thought about when I wore this dress on our wedding day."

His gaze drifted over her. "And you're more beautiful now than you were then."

She moved to stand in front of him. "I'm glad you think so." She frowned at the sadness in his eyes. "How did it go with the sheriff?"

He gave a disgusted grunt. "About like I expected. He brushed the whole episode aside as if it didn't matter. 'After all,' he said, 'it was just a former slave that probably was stealing from somebody, and they decided to teach him a lesson.'"

Savannah's mouth gaped open, and she shook the brush she still held in his face. "Teach him a lesson? By killing him?"

"That's what I said, but the sheriff told me to go on home and let him worry about keeping the peace in the community."

Savannah clenched her fists and stomped her foot on the floor. "He hasn't worried about that since the day he took office. Oh, I'd like to teach him a lesson."

Dante's tired eyes flickered with laughter. "Remind me never to make you mad, my dear."

Savannah's face burned, and she turned away. "Quit teasing me and get dressed. I laid your clothes out."

He followed her to the bed where his Sunday suit lay. He wrapped his arms around her waist and pulled her against him. His warm breath fanned her neck. "Thank you, Savannah."

She twisted in his arms and turned to face him. "For what?"

His arms tightened, and he bent his head. "For being my wife."

Her lips met his in a sweet kiss that set her head spinning.

She pulled back and smiled at him. "We're going to be late for the funeral."

He chuckled and released her. "The voice of reason has spoken. I'll change clothes."

She placed the brush on the dresser and headed for the door. "I'm going back to Mamie's. Come on over when you get ready." She stopped and whirled to face him before she left. "Oh, I forgot. Did you get the extra guns?"

"I did."

A frown pulled at her brow. "That probably ran our bill up a lot at the store. Can we afford it?"

He sank down on the side of the bed and ran his fingers through his hair. "We can if we have a good crop next year. Right now I have to do everything I can to protect our home."

She nodded. "Yes, you're right."

He didn't move or respond to her words. His head drooped, and his shoulders sagged. Last night's events had touched him deeply. Savannah wished she could take some of the worry from his shoulders. Since their marriage, she'd come to a new understanding. God had a way of helping His children see what was most important in life. Money, land, acceptance in the community weren't bad things to have, but without love and family, they meant nothing.

Once she thought being back at Cottonwood was the only thing that would make her happy. Now she realized that her parents and all the people who'd lived on the plantation were what had given her home true meaning.

The land and her goal of returning it to its former glory now took second place in her life to the man she had come to love. For the first time in her life, she had her priorities in the right order. She finally understood that it was the people she loved and who loved her that made life worth living.

fifteen

Savannah glanced up from the shirt she was mending and stared at Mamie, who sat across the table from her. Three months had passed since they'd buried Abraham in the small cemetery where Cottonwood slaves had been buried for years, but Mamie still had not recovered.

Savannah laid her sewing aside and reached across the table to grasp Mamie's hand. "Mamie, can I get you something to drink?"

Mamie shook her head. "No, thanks, Miss 'Vanna. I'm fine."

Savannah rose and knelt beside Mamie's chair. "But I'm worried about you. You hardly eat anything. You've got to take care of yourself better."

A tear ran down Mamie's cheek. "I knows that, but it's hard to do."

"Saul and Joshua love you. They're concerned, too."

Mamie nodded. "I know, but I can't get over seeing my baby dead. That ain't 'posed to happen. Chil'run shouldn't die 'fore they mamma and poppa do."

"I understand how you feel, but—"

Mamie held up a hand. "No, you don't know how I feel, but you will soon when your baby come."

Savannah's eyebrows arched, and she stared at Mamie. "I told you that's a long time off."

A smile curled Mamie's face. "Don't you knows you got life in you, Miss 'Vanna?"

Savannah pushed to her feet and stared down at Mamie. "What are you talking about?"

Mamie rose from her chair and pressed her hand to Savannah's stomach. "You with child, Miss 'Vanna. I knowed it some time ago. I reckon we be seeing your baby born this fall."

The breath left Savannah's body. "No. You can't be serious."

Mamie nodded. "It true. You and Mistuh Dante gwine have a baby, and we gwine see new life on Cottonwood. I 'spect Mistuh Dante be right proud."

Savannah's mind whirled with thoughts she'd tried to dismiss for weeks. The tiredness, the queasy stomach in the mornings, and small changes she'd noticed in her body. They all added up to what she'd ignored. She was going to be a mother.

Her eyes grew wide. "Do you really think I'm going to have a baby?"

"I knows you are. I can always tell."

"B—but why didn't I know?"

Mamie chuckled. "I reckon you would real soon."

Savannah opened her mouth to protest, but the words wouldn't come. Laughter rippled through her body, and she threw her arms around Mamie and hugged her. "I'm going to be a mother."

"Yas'm. And Mistuh Dante be a poppa."

At the mention of her husband, Savannah froze. Although there had been no raids on Cottonwood, rumors circulated that the band of murderers who attacked the Crossroads community still roamed the countryside from time to time. She didn't want to add a wife who was going to have a baby to his worries, but he needed to know.

"Don't tell Dante about this yet."

Mamie frowned. "But why? He the father."

"I know, but he's been so worried about what's been happening in the countryside. He's gone into town today to talk to the sheriff. I'll tell him when the time is right. Just not yet. Promise me?"

Mamie's eyes clouded, but she nodded. "All right, Miss 'Vanna. You tell him when you gets ready."

The cabin door flew open, and Dante strode into the room. Savannah could tell from the expression on his face something was wrong.

Mamie gathered up her sewing and hurried to the door. "I gots to get home. Saul be coming from the barn soon. I'll see you later, Miss 'Vanna." She nodded to Dante. "Mistuh Dante."

He smiled at Mamie. "Take care of yourself, Mamie."

Dante closed the door when Mamie left and shrugged his coat from his shoulders. Savannah watched as he hung it up and trudged to the table.

"What's the matter?"

He sat down and motioned for her to do the same. "I want to talk to you."

The tone of his voice frightened her. She eased into the chair. "Dante, you're scaring me."

He clasped his hands on the table in front of him. "I hope I'm wrong, but I'm afraid we may have a visit from the raiders this evening."

Her heart pounded, and she swallowed back the fear that rose in her throat. "What makes you think they'd come now? It's been three months since Abraham's death, and they haven't bothered us."

"It was the attitude of the sheriff today. When I asked him what he'd found out about Abraham's lynching, he told me that anybody who would get upset over somebody hanging a thief might need to think about protecting his own home." His fist pounded the table, and Savannah jumped in surprise. "He knows who they are, Savannah. He as much as said so. For all I know, he could be one of them, too."

"What makes you think it could be tonight?"

He shrugged. "Tonight, tomorrow, the next night—I don't know. But we have to be prepared. I've told the men what I need them to do. Now I want you to listen to me and do as I say."

"What is it?"

He sat up straighter. "If they come, they may set fire to the cabins like they did at the Crossroads, so I don't want anybody in them. I want you to take the women and children to the woods. The men and I will stay hidden here. After all, they believe they're coming after former slaves who wouldn't dare fight back against a white man. We intend to show them differently. With any luck, we'll be able to surprise them."

Her heart pounded in fear, but she didn't want Dante to see that she was afraid. She pushed back from the table and headed toward the stove. "That sounds like a good idea. I'll fix you something to eat. Then I'll get the women."

He followed her and turned her toward him. "Tell the women to take plenty of quilts to keep warm. The nights are still cold."

"I will."

"I'll do everything I can to protect Cottonwood, Savannah. Just take care of yourself."

"You do the same, Dante." Tears burned her eyes. "I can't stand the thought of anything happening to you."

He slid his arms around her and drew her close. The muscle in his jaw twitched as he stared into her eyes. "I love you, Savannah."

After a moment, he released his hold on her and walked toward the sideboard. With a sigh she directed her gaze back to the stove and reached for the frying pan. When she looked over her shoulder, he pulled the pistol from the sideboard drawer.

He walked back to the table and laid it down. "Take this and some ammunition with you. Shoot anybody who threatens you or any of the others."

The frying pan slipped from her shaking fingers and clattered as it struck the stove top. "S–shoot them?"

His eyebrows arched. "Do you know how to shoot a gun?"

Fear knotted her stomach as she remembered when and why she'd learned to use a gun. This situation was no different from that one then "My father taught me in case we ever had to defend Cottonwood during the war."

His lips thinned. "Be careful, Savannah, but if you feel any of you are in danger, shoot to kill."

She stared into his eyes. "I will."

❧

Savannah didn't think she'd ever been so cold in her life. Her stomach rumbled, and she shook her head in disgust. Nausea had kept her from eating all day, but now wasn't the time to be thinking about food. She had to concentrate on something else and get her mind off her hunger.

A cold wind blew through the woods where she and the women and their children hid. They'd been lucky to find a dry place where they could sit and huddle underneath the covers they'd brought. Time had passed slowly since they'd left home hours ago. They'd trudged deep into the forest before stopping. Now they sat silent, hoping that someone would soon come and tell them it was safe to go back home.

Her thoughts turned to Dante, and she wondered where

he was. She glanced over at Mamie, who sat on a fallen log, her back straight and her body unmoving. The other women sat silently with their children gathered close.

Savannah pulled her quilt tighter and settled against a tree trunk. She touched the barrel of the gun that protruded from her coat pocket. Fatigue washed over her, and she closed her eyes for a moment. Blinking, she straightened. She couldn't go to sleep. Dante expected her to protect everyone.

She closed her eyes again and hovered on the brink of sleep. A rebel yell pierced the quiet night, and Savannah bolted upright. The other women sat up, but no one said a word. Savannah breathed a prayer of thanks that none of the children had awakened.

Fear radiated from the small group as Savannah strained to hear any distant sounds. Another yell split the air. Then gunshots from the direction of Cottonwood blasted through the night. Savannah's stomach roiled.

The gunshots echoed through the forest for several minutes. Then a deadly calm descended, leaving a silence so eerie that the hairs on the back of her neck prickled. All kinds of thoughts ran through her mind. She could imagine the men from Cottonwood lying in the cabin clearing—all dead from trying to protect the place they called home.

Savannah threw the quilt back and rose to her feet. She glanced around at the women, who huddled protectively near their children. "I'm going to walk to the edge of the forest and see if I can tell what's going on. Don't leave until I get back."

Without waiting for an answer, she hurried in the direction they'd come when they entered the forest. If she could just get to the edge, maybe she would be able to tell what had happened.

The closer she came to the field beyond the woods, the slower her steps became. She stopped before stepping out into the open and gazed toward home. She couldn't make out the cabins in the distance, but at least there were no fires that she could see.

Pounding hoofbeats alerted her to a rider coming toward her. In the dark, she couldn't tell who it was, but she hoped it was Dante coming to bring them back home. She pulled the gun from her pocket and stepped closer to the forest's edge.

Too late she realized she'd moved right into the path of the horse. She screamed, and the rider pulled back on the reins. The horse reared, his hoofs beating at the air as the rider attempted to get the animal under control. When the horse settled, the rider pulled his gun.

"I hear you in there. Come on out before I start shooting."

Savannah flinched at the sound of Jonathan's voice, and she stepped from behind the tree. Jonathan, a white hood covering his face, sat on his horse, which still pranced in place.

"Jonathan, what are you doing? Have you lost your mind?"

"Savannah?" The words sounded muffled under the hood.

"Why have you turned into a killer and a traitor to your own people?"

He laughed. "Traitor? You're a fine one to talk. I loved you, Savannah, and you left me for a yellow coward who stole your land."

"You never loved me. You loved my family's land."

He shook his head, and the hood swayed. "You're wrong. I loved you, but I waited too long to tell you. You'd already deceived me and married that carpetbagger."

"Don't talk about Dante like that."

"He's no good for you, Savannah. He can't have you."

She backed up a step. "What do you mean?"

He pulled his gun from his holster. "You're a traitor to your people. I'm going to kill you."

Fear gripped Savannah at the sight of the gun aimed at her. Before she had time to think, she raised her hand and fired. The first shot went over Jonathan's head, and the horse reared up again. As he wrestled with the reins, she fired a second shot, and he dropped his gun and cried out in pain.

Jonathan grabbed his leg and bent over the saddle. "You haven't heard the last of me." He jerked the reins and dug his heels into the horse's side.

She watched Jonathan disappear into the night before she collapsed against a tree. Tears ran down her face. She looked at the gun in her hand and replaced it in her coat pocket.

After a few moments, she turned to reenter the forest, but a light across the open field caught her attention. The flickering flame bounced up and down. It had to be a lantern, and whoever was holding it was running.

She pulled the gun out, stepped behind a tree, and stared as the light came closer. A yellow glow from the flame reflected off the face of Dante, and she cried out in relief.

"Dante!"

Savannah ran toward him and threw herself into his arms. His arms encircled her and pulled her close. "Savannah. Are you all right? I heard gunshots." His voice trembled.

She pulled away from him and stared up into his face. "I had to see what was going on. Jonathan found me."

He set the lantern on the ground and held her at arm's length. "Are you certain it was Boyer?"

"I recognized his voice. He hates me for marrying you and wanted to kill me. So I shot him first."

"Did you kill him?"

"I think I just hit him in the leg. But tell me what happened."

He picked up the lantern. "We were able to hold them off. I think we wounded a few. So I've come to take all of you home."

"Good. Let's go get the women and children. They're so cold."

Savannah turned to head back the way she'd come, but Dante grabbed her arm. She glanced over her shoulder at him.

"I'm sorry your friends have turned against you because of me, Savannah."

The sad look on his face told her he meant what he said. She shook her head. "The friends who really count have accepted you. Jonathan's still fighting the war, and I can't do anything about that."

Dante took a deep breath. "Then let's go bring our people home."

She smiled and led the way into the forest. The thought of how she'd thrown herself into Dante's arms returned, and her skin grew warm. She'd never known anyone who had the power to calm her fears like he could. Her heart filled with love for him. Now they needed to build their life together without worrying about protecting their land.

sixteen

Dante walked to the bedroom door and looked in on Savannah. After all the excitement of the night before, he'd let her sleep this morning. She'd been exhausted when they got home, and he'd thought she'd go right to bed. She'd surprised him, though, by saying that she had to eat something first. He could hardly believe all she consumed before finally falling into bed.

Now that he thought about it, he didn't remember seeing her eat anything earlier yesterday. He'd never seen her that hungry before.

He stepped back into the kitchen and poured himself another cup of coffee and opened his Bible. The quiet in the early morning hours provided the best time for reading and studying God's Word. He opened the book and found himself transported to another time and place where a young man faced a giant with a sling.

From time to time he took a sip from the cup and had just drained the last drop when he heard Savannah stirring in the bedroom. He started to get up and pour himself another cup of coffee, but he froze at the sound of running footsteps. Savannah, still in her gown and her long hair falling on her shoulders, dashed by him and out the cabin door.

Surprised at her hasty departure, he set the cup on the table, walked to the front door, and peered outside. He couldn't see her, but he could hear her beside the cabin and knew she was in the process of losing everything she'd eaten the night before.

At a loss about what to do to help her, he glanced into the cabin. The quilt she'd taken to the woods the night before lay draped over a chair. He grabbed it and went outside. When he stepped around the corner, his heart pricked at the sight of her leaning against the cabin.

He draped the quilt around her, and she looked over her shoulder and smiled. "Thanks."

Her pallor frightened him. The cheeks that were usually rosy were pale this morning, and her eyes drooped at the corners. "Are you all right?"

She nodded. "I'm better now." She pushed into a standing position but lurched toward him.

Surprised, he scooped her into his arms and carried her back into the cabin. When they got to the bedroom, he laid her on the bed and covered her up. "Last night really didn't agree with you. I think you should stay in bed today."

She pushed up on her elbows. "I'm fine now, Dante. I have too much to do to stay in bed."

He restrained her. "You heard me. You're to stay in bed until you're feeling better. Now is there anything I can get you? Some coffee maybe?"

Her face screwed into a grimace. "The thought of coffee makes me sick. Maybe I'll feel like eating something later."

He stared down at her for a moment. "I have to go into town and tell the sheriff what happened last night. I'll ask Mamie to look in on you."

Savannah shook her head. "No, she's had too much happen in the last few days. I'll be fine. By the time you get back, I should be up and feeling better."

He hesitated. He didn't want to leave, but the sheriff needed to be informed about what had happened. "Well, if you're sure, I'll come back as quickly as possible."

"I'm sure. Now go on."

Dante turned to the door, but he glanced back at her once more. She'd already closed her eyes.

He didn't like leaving her alone when she was ill. All kinds of thoughts tumbled through his head. She might need something and be unable to call out. Or she could get up, faint, and hit her head on something. She could lie there for hours before anybody came to check on her. No matter what she said, he was going to ask Mamie to look in on her in a few hours.

If anything happened to her, he didn't know what he'd do.

❧

The sheriff leaned back in his chair, propped his feet on his desk, and pulled a knife from his pocket. Opening it, he began to clean under his fingernails. He didn't look up at Dante. "How do you know it was Jonathan Boyer? Did you see him?"

Dante tried to control his growing anger at the sheriff. Ever since he'd arrived and told his story of the raid at Cottonwood, the man had come up with excuses why Dante couldn't possibly be sure of the identity of the men behind the masks.

Dante inhaled and tried once more. "I didn't see him, but my wife recognized his voice. She's known him all her life."

The sheriff laughed. "Scared women think they hear a lot of things in the dark. It could have been anybody who sounded like him."

"No. He threatened her and said things only Boyer knew."

"Well, tell you what I'll do. First chance I get, I'll ride out to Oak Hill and question Mr. Boyer. After all, he ain't goin' nowhere. He wouldn't leave his plantation."

Dante walked around the desk and shoved the sheriff's feet to the floor. He bent over until their noses almost touched. "Now I'll tell you what I'm going to do. First chance I get, like maybe this afternoon, I'm going to ride over to Selma and talk to the federal officials there. I'm sure they'll be interested in a sheriff who allows murderers to roam the countryside, killing freed slaves and terrorizing landowners."

The sheriff tried to push up, but the back legs of the chair slipped out from under him, and he tipped backward. His face red with rage, he struggled to get to his feet. "Don't threaten me, you carpetbagger."

Dante looked down at him and grimaced. "You disgust me. You're supposed to protect the people of this county, and you take the side of the lawbreakers. You deserve everything you're about to get."

Dante strode from the room and slammed the door behind him. He shook with anger. How that man ever attained the office of sheriff was beyond Dante. The man was an insult to the office of law enforcer.

After a moment, he took a deep breath and headed toward the general store. Maybe he could find something that would make Savannah feel better.

A bell over the door tinkled when Dante stepped into the store. Mr. Perkins, the owner, stood at a counter rearranging bolts of cloth. He glanced up and smiled. "Mr. Rinaldi, come in. How're things out your way today?"

"Not so good, I'm afraid. Cottonwood was raided last night."

The man's eyes grew wide. "Anybody hurt?"

"Not any of our people, but a few of our visitors may have been hit. I wonder if anybody's come to see Dr. Spencer today with a gunshot wound."

Mr. Perkins shook his head. "I don't know. Doc hasn't been in here. If I hear anything, I'll let you know." The man pushed one last bolt of cloth into place and stepped back to eye the display. He turned toward the door as the bell tinkled again. "Come in, Mrs. Thompson."

Dante glanced over his shoulder to see Martha Thompson entering. He wondered what gossip she was peddling this morning. He tried to smile. "Good morning, Mrs. Thompson. It's good to see you again."

"You, too, Mr. Rinaldi." She walked over to the counter and picked up a bolt of the material Mr. Perkins had just arranged and laid it on a table behind her. "Now don't you worry about me, Mr. Perkins. You help Mr. Rinaldi, and I'll just make myself at home while I look at this bolt at the bottom of the stack."

Mr. Perkins's eyebrows arched, and he motioned for Dante to follow him. "If you need anything, let me know." He turned to Dante. "Now what can I help you with?"

"I'm looking for something for my wife."

"Like a present?"

Dante shook his head. "No, she isn't feeling well. I thought I might be able to get some tonic."

Mr. Perkins pointed to a shelf that contained medicine bottles. Dante peered at the labels—some marked tonics, others elixirs. "I don't know which one."

"What are her symptoms?"

Dante searched his mind and realized that Savannah hadn't felt well in several weeks. Although she hadn't complained, he understood now that she was sick. Fear welled up in him. What if it was something serious? Perhaps he should rush home and bring her back to see Dr. Spencer.

"She tires very easily, doesn't have much energy. She's very pale, and her appetite is gone. This morning she lost everything she'd eaten last night." Reciting the symptoms scared him even more, and he turned to Mr. Perkins. "Do you think it could be something serious?"

Before he could answer, a shrill laugh pierced his ears. He turned to see Martha Thompson shaking her head and laughing as if she'd just heard the funniest joke of her life. "Oh you men," she cackled. "You're about as useless as a sick hound dog."

Dante frowned and walked toward her. "What's so funny?"

She roared with laughter again. "You are. And you call yourself a husband."

Dante glanced back at Mr. Perkins, who appeared to be as mystified as he. "I'm sorry, Mrs. Thompson, I have no idea what you're talking about."

She pulled a handkerchief from her pocket and wiped at the tears that streaked her face. "I ain't even a doctor, and I know exactly what's wrong with your wife 'cause I've had the same symptoms five times now."

Dante stared at the woman, who looked healthy. If Savannah and Mrs. Thompson shared the same disease, it must not be fatal. "Then would you mind telling me what it is?"

Martha grinned. "Nothing that nine months won't take care of."

He frowned. "What are you talking. . . ?" His voice trailed off as the meaning of her words dawned on him. "Are you saying. . . ?"

Martha smile and nodded. "Congratulations, Mr. Rinaldi."

Dante glanced over his shoulder at Mr. Perkins. "I—I think I'd better go. I'll come back later."

Without waiting for an answer, Dante rushed from the store and ran to the hitching post where he'd left his horse. Untying the reins, he jumped into the saddle and turned his horse toward Cottonwood. Once outside of town, he nudged the horse into a gallop.

The wind burned his face, but he hardly noticed. All he could think about was that he was going to be a father, but that wasn't the best part. He and Savannah would have something that would bind them together for the rest of their lives.

seventeen

Savannah ate the last bite of biscuit and took a sip from her cup. The molasses she'd stirred into the coffee gave it a sweet taste and eased the queasiness in her stomach. She placed her dishes in the dry sink and glanced around the small room.

For the first time, she wondered what it had been like for the slaves who'd lived in this cabin. When she was growing up, she'd hardly given thought to the plight of the people who labored for her family. Now she called this dilapidated house her home, and she understood how bad it must have been for the families who lived in the shadow of the big house.

The small cabin provided just enough space for two people. With the baby, they would be crowded, but they could do it. After all, Mamie and Saul and their two sons shared a cabin just a bit larger than theirs, but their home probably seemed very empty now with Abraham gone.

A knock at the door interrupted her thoughts, and she hurried to open it. Mamie stood on the porch. Her eyes were swollen from crying, but she smiled at Savannah. "How you doin', Miss 'Vanna?"

Savannah reached out and drew the woman inside. She put her arms around Mamie and hugged her. "I'm feeling better. How are you today?"

Mamie sighed. "I 'spects I've been better. I just gotta put this in the Lord's hands and try to get on with my life. I still got Saul and Joshua, and I be thankful for that."

Savannah blinked back tears. "You're a strong woman, Mamie. You'll never get over missing Abraham, but you'll come to a point where you can remember the good times you had with him and be thankful for that."

"Yas'm. I knows that. But I come over to see how you feelin'. Mistuh Dante asked me to check on you, and that's what I'm doin'."

Savannah smiled. "I just ate something, and I'm feeling much better."

Mamie arched one eyebrow. "You ain't tole Mistuh Dante yet, have you?"

Savannah shook her head. "I've tried to, but he's had so much on his mind with all that's happened I didn't want to add to it."

"You have to tell him soon. Cain't keep a secret like this long."

Savannah drew the woman toward the stove and pulled out a chair for her. They sat down, and Savannah basked in the warmth before she turned to Mamie. "I'm afraid, Mamie."

A look of surprise flashed on Mamie's face. "Why you 'fraid?"

Savannah sat up straight. "What if I'm not a good mother?"

Mamie chuckled. "Oh Miss 'Vanna, you be fine. Lots of women feel that way 'fore their first baby born, but don't you worry none. I been knowin' you since you was born, and you gwine make a good mamma."

"What makes you so sure? I've never taken care of a baby before."

"You can do anything you set your mind to. Just look what you and Mistuh Dante already done. You come back to Cottonwood all ready to make it a grand plantation again, but you not like the girl who left it when the big house burn. You come back with a good man who loves you a lot. I'd shore like to see his face when you tell him about the baby."

Savannah smiled. "You really think he'll be happy?"

"I don't think. I knows it. I thought that poor man gwine go crazy when he heard you want to go on that boat down to Mobile. He couldn't eat or sleep. I knowed all along what he needed to do, so I tole him there was a way to keep you here. And he did it. He got up his nerve and asked you to marry him. When he tole me you done accepted him, he was the happiest man I ever seen." Mamie rose from her chair. "Now you gwine make him so happy he shout."

Savannah laughed and followed Mamie to the door. "Thank you, Mamie. You've always been the one to help me when I needed it. Now I have to decide how I'm going to tell Dante." She stepped onto the front porch and inhaled. "It may be chilly, but it's a beautiful day. I do my best thinking at my parents' graves. I'm going to put my coat on and walk down there."

Mamie smiled and walked down the steps. Savannah stared after her until she had disappeared into her home. Then she reentered the cabin and pulled her coat from the peg by the door. A visit to the cemetery often provided her peace and guidance. She hoped today would be no exception.

She picked up her Bible and started to leave. A warning niggled in the back of her mind. With all the turmoil in the countryside, she probably shouldn't venture so far without protection. She walked to the sideboard, pulled the pistol from the drawer, and stuck it in her pocket.

❧

Dante reined the horse to a stop at Cottonwood's barn and dismounted. He'd ridden harder than he should to get home, but he couldn't wait to see Savannah. One glance at the lather on the mare, though, told him the horse had to be taken care of first.

He led the horse into the alleyway of the barn and pulled the saddle and blanket from its back. A voice from behind startled him.

"Mistuh Dante, I didn't know you got back."

Dante turned to see Saul walking out of one of the stalls at the far end of the barn. "I finished my business and hurried home. I didn't want to leave Savannah alone too long."

Saul stopped beside him and pulled the tattered hat from his head. "She ain't home right now. Mamie went over to check on her awhile ago, and she said she gwine go visit her folks at the cemetery."

Dante frowned. "Did she walk?"

"Yas suh, I thinks so."

The flicker of anger he'd held back on the ride home ignited. She'd kept the news of his child from him, and now she was out walking by herself. After last night's scare, she should have stayed inside like he told her.

Saul coughed, and Dante jerked his attention back to the man beside him. "I'm sorry, Saul. I have a lot on my mind."

"Yas suh."

He handed the reins of the horse to Saul. "Would you mind taking care of my horse? I need to go see my wife."

Saul took the reins and smiled. "I 'spects it 'bout time you got things straightened out in your house, Mistuh Dante."

Dante's eyes grew wide. "Do you know something that I don't? Like the fact that I'm about to become a father, and my wife hasn't told me?"

A sad smile curled Saul's lips. "Yas suh. Miss 'Vanna done tole Mamie, and Mamie tole me. I 'spect it be a happy time here at Cottonwood. The good Lord took away Abraham, but He done give us a new life to bless us. He has a way of makin' things right even when bad things happen."

Dante stared at him. "You can say that with faith after the horrible death of your son?"

Tears filled Saul's eyes. "I thought losing my mamma when I was little was the worstest that could ever happen, but I was wrong. I ain't never gwine git over Abraham, but the Lord done tole me He be right there a-helpin' me each day."

"I know that Saul, but thank you for reminding me."

Dante squared his shoulders and strode toward the river. When he reached the bluff, he stared down into the rolling water and remembered the first night he'd come to Cottonwood and how he'd lain under the stars and listened to its lull. In the time since then, he'd come to love every inch of soil on his land.

Savannah had told him she wanted her child to inherit Cottonwood. Now she said she loved him, but he wondered how she would feel after the baby was born. It scared him to think now that she had what she'd wanted, she would no longer need him.

❧

Savannah could tell from the sun's position she'd been in the cemetery for several hours. She rose to her feet and closed her Bible. Glancing down at the graves once more, she put her fingers to her lips and blew a kiss to the parents she loved.

She left the small burial ground and walked along the path in deep thought until she approached the bend that brought her to the river's edge. She stopped on the tall bluff and stared at the water far below.

Once she had wanted to travel the steamboats that plowed this river, but no more. She had found contentment at Cottonwood with Dante. Guilt over her silence about the baby filled her. Even if Dante was worried about the protection of everyone living on the plantation, she had to tell him. It wasn't fair to keep it from him anymore.

The sound of a snapping twig caught her attention. She turned to look behind her. Maybe one of the men had been to the canebrake they'd cleared and was coming back, but she saw no one. Turning to continue home, she jerked to a halt and swallowed the fear rising in her throat. Jonathan Boyer blocked her path.

"Jonathan, what are you doing here?"

His lips curled into a snarl, and he glared at her with hatred. He limped forward. "I came to see you, Savannah." He stopped and grimaced in pain.

She glanced down at his leg. "Are you hurt?"

"Hurt? Don't you remember shooting me last night? You didn't think I'd recovered already, did you?"

She walked closer. "I'm sorry, Jonathan. I didn't want to hurt you. Let me get you back to my house, and I'll send for Dr. Spencer."

He held out his hand to stop her. "Don't you come near me. Because of you and your husband, I've lost everything I ever wanted. Cottonwood, you, and now Oak Hill."

She frowned. "I don't understand. How have you lost Oak Hill?"

He flinched and shifted his weight to the other leg. "Your dear husband made a visit to the sheriff this morning and threatened to go to the federal authorities if he didn't do something. So our good law officer decided he'd better get busy before that happened."

Savannah backed up a step. "What did Sheriff Newton do?"

"He went over to Sam Baker's place and told him he knew Sam was one of the people who attacked the Crossroads. He promised Sam he'd overlook his bad judgment in joining the raiders if he'd disclose the names of everybody in the group. So Sam talked. He told the sheriff how we raided the countryside and how we hung that slave Abraham. Now the sheriff's after me for murder. I expect he wants to hang me so it'll look good for him."

"Then you need to give yourself up. It may go better with you if you go in voluntarily."

He glanced up at the sky and laughed. "You must think I'm crazy. I'm going to finish what I started last night. Then I'm leaving Alabama and everything in it far behind."

Jonathan's laugh sent chills up Savannah's spine. It had the tone of a deranged man. "Please, Jonathan, let me help you."

"Yes, my dear. You're going to help me a lot. I'm going to make your husband wish he'd never come to Alabama."

He stuck his hand into his pocket and whipped out a knife as he advanced on her. Savannah stared in horror at the long blade flashing in the sun. She backed up a step. "Jonathan, what are you doing?"

"You should never have turned against me, Savannah. Now I'm going to kill you."

She wanted to run, but her body seemed frozen in place. The hatred burning in his eyes told her this wasn't the friend she'd always known. She screamed as he advanced, then she pulled the gun from her pocket and fired.

eighteen

A woman's scream followed by a gunshot sent an icy chill down Dante's back. It had to be Savannah's voice he heard. He hesitated for only a moment before he bolted in the direction of the sounds.

Near the bend in the road ahead, he saw a man with a knife raised above his head. The man staggered forward, his attention directed to someone in front of him.

"Stay back, Jonathan!" Dante heard Savannah yell. "I'll aim lower next time!"

Dante sprinted forward and grabbed Jonathan's upraised arm. A few feet away, he could see Savannah with a pistol in her hand.

Jonathan whirled in Dante's grip and stared at him. Dante almost felt the heat from the hatred that burned in Jonathan's eyes. Grimacing, Jonathan struggled to free himself from Dante's grip.

"Let me go. I'll kill you both."

Dante could feel Jonathan weakening, and he remembered Savannah had said she shot him the night before. With a new burst of strength, Dante gripped Jonathan's wrist tighter and twisted it away from his body. The knife dropped to the ground.

Letting go of Jonathan's arm, Dante drew back his fist and connected with his assailant's jaw. Jonathan lurched back and fell to the ground. Dante stood over him, but Jonathan didn't move.

Dante turned to Savannah. "Are you all right?"

She bit her lower lip and nodded. "I'm fine. I'm so glad you got here when you did. I don't know what—" Her eyes widened in fear. "Dante," she screamed, "look out!"

Dante whirled to see Jonathan approaching with a large rock held above his head. "I'm not through yet."

Dante ducked, grabbed Jonathan around the waist, and propelled him backward to the edge of the bluff. The ground crumbled underneath their feet, and dirt and rocks rolled down the steep bank toward the river. Dante tried to pull back, but Jonathan gripped him tighter.

A large crack appeared in the earth between Dante's and Jonathan's feet. Dante released his hold, swung his fists up, and hit Jonathan's arms. The force knocked Jonathan loose, and he shifted his weight to swing again. Dante stepped back to avoid the blow he knew was coming.

Before Jonathan could deliver the punch, the edge of the bluff collapsed beneath him. His arms flailed as he struggled to regain his balance, but his footing had disappeared in the earth that slid down the bluff toward the river.

Dante reached for Jonathan, but it was too late. He fell back, tumbling downward amid the rocks and dirt. Dante watched the man's body twist and turn until it came to rest at the edge of the river, far below.

A sob next to him alerted Dante that Savannah stood there.

"Oh Jonathan, what happened to the boy I knew?"

Dante turned to her. "It was the war, Savannah. Maybe those who died were luckier than the ones who survived."

She tilted her head. "What do you mean?"

"Men like Jonathan couldn't accept the changes in the South and in their lives. It must have eaten away at him until it destroyed the boy you knew." His shoulders drooped. "I never meant to kill him, though. I hope you believe that."

Her eyes sparkled with tears. "I do."

"Mistuh Dante, Mistuh Dante, what going on here?"

They turned at the sound of Saul's voice. He ran toward them with Big Mike and Henry Walton right behind. When they reached the edge of the bluff, Dante pointed downward. "Jonathan Boyer came back. He's down there."

Saul stared at the body below. "That the man who killed Abraham?"

Savannah nodded. "Yes. He confessed to me."

Saul took a deep breath. "Then let's bring him up."

Dante clamped his hand on Saul's shoulder. "We will. Then I'll take the body into town to the sheriff and tell him what happened."

Savannah reached out and touched Dante's arm. "Do you want me to go with you?"

He shook his head. "No. You go on home. I'll see you there when I get back. We have some things to settle between us."

She wiped at a tear that escaped her eye. "I suppose we do."

She straightened her shoulders and walked down the path toward home. He watched her for a few moments before he remembered the men who were already climbing down the bluff to recover Jonathan's body.

When he bought Cottonwood, he had hopes of finding the happiness he'd been wanting for years. Now he had the land and a wife who said she loved him, but he also had to face the fact that he'd forced Savannah to marry him and then had killed the man she might have married. They had a lot to talk about when he got back from town.

❧

The last rays of sunlight dotted the horizon when Dante stepped onto the cabin's porch hours later. The time at Sheriff Newton's office had taken much longer than he expected, but he'd finally been allowed to leave. Thanks to the questioning of Sam Baker earlier in the day, Dante's accounts of Jonathan's death and of Savannah's presence at the scene compelled the sheriff to accept Dante's statement. He had returned home, but a more difficult task lay before him.

On the ride back from town, he'd pondered what he was going to say to Savannah. He knew from the beginning she only married him for the plantation, but he thought that had all changed. She'd said she loved him. But did she really mean it? If she did, why hadn't she told him they were going to have a baby?

Dante pounded his fist against the post at the edge of the porch. It was time he found out.

He pushed the cabin door open and had no sooner stepped inside than Savannah appeared in the bedroom doorway. She'd already lit the lamps, and the flickering flames about the room cast a glow over her. The anger he'd felt a few minutes before dissolved at the sight of her waiting to welcome him home.

She smiled and hurried forward. "Let me help you with your coat." She moved behind him and pulled the heavy coat from his shoulders. When it slipped from his arms, she turned and hung it next to the door. "Now sit down at the table. I have your supper ready. You've hardly eaten anything today and must be starved."

He grabbed her arm before she could head to the stove. "Eating can wait, Savannah. I think we need to talk."

Her lips trembled. "About what?"

He led her to the kitchen table and pulled out a chair. "Sit down. There are some things we need to settle between us."

Her eyes grew wide, but she eased into the chair without looking away from him. "You sound so serious, Dante. If it's about Jonathan, I want you to know his death wasn't your fault. He came here looking for trouble and meant for us to die. It's because of his actions that he's dead."

Dante sat across from her, stretched his arms out on the table, and balled his fists. "I've tried to tell myself that, but the fact remains he still died at my hands."

She reached across and covered his hands with hers. "Don't think like that. It wasn't your fault."

His skin burned from her touch, and he pulled his hands away. "I've thought a lot today about Jonathan's state of mind. I know he came back nursing horrible memories of the war, but many of us did. Maybe it was more than that. I think he loved you, and his anger turned to violence when I made you marry me."

A look of surprise flashed across her face. "You didn't make me marry you, Dante. I agreed."

He nodded. "Yes, you did. But you never would have married me if I hadn't dangled Cottonwood in front of you."

She straightened in her chair and frowned. "Are you saying that you're sorry you married me?"

"I'm saying that everybody around here thought of me as a foreigner and a carpetbagger. There's no way you would have agreed unless there was something in it for you, and that something was Cottonwood."

Tears pooled in her eyes, and she pushed to her feet. "It's a little late to be reliving the past, isn't it? All you wanted was to be accepted in the community, to have friends. You already had Cottonwood. In time, the people around here would have gotten to know you, and you would have been accepted. When you proposed, I couldn't understand why you would give me so much when you were really getting so little in return."

He stood and faced her. "I told you why, Savannah. I couldn't get you out of my mind from the moment you almost ran me down with that buggy. It was afterward, though, when I saw you here at your parents' graves and witnessed how you tended your sick aunt that I knew I loved you like I would never love another. I thought I'd go crazy when you said you were leaving. I had to find a way to stop you. I knew the only thing that would keep you here would be Cottonwood, and I was right. I used your love for Cottonwood to get what I wanted. I'm sorry for doing that."

Savannah exhaled a long breath. "I'm not sorry."

Dante frowned. "You're not?"

She took his right hand in both of hers, brought it to her mouth, and kissed it. Still holding it close to her lips, she glanced up. "If you had let me go, I never would have known the happiness I've had from loving you. I told myself I was marrying you to come home to Cottonwood, but I think I was only deceiving myself. I think I fell in love with you that first day, too. It just took me longer to realize it."

His heart pounded in his chest so hard he could barely breathe. "I know you said you love me, but I've scarce let myself believe it. Are you sure?"

"I am." Savannah still held his hand, and she cupped it in both of hers. "Why is it so difficult for you to believe that I love you?"

He swallowed. "I haven't had anybody who loved me in a long time, Savannah. I've been so lonely, and I didn't dare dream that a beautiful woman like you could see anything worth loving in a man like me."

"Oh Dante. I never realized how lonely you were, but you're not anymore. I'm here with you, and I love you with all my heart." Savannah took a deep breath. "But I think we need to make some changes around here. We need to do what we should have done when we first married. We need to voice our feelings to each other."

"I think you're right." He wrapped his arms around her. "I know we've already stood before a preacher, but I want to start this marriage over. Let's forget about business propositions and concentrate on loving each other. What do you think?"

She nodded. "I don't remember much of what Reverend Somers said the day of our wedding. So I think I should make some new vows to you."

"W—what kind of vows?"

A smile pulled at her lips. "You're the best man I've ever known, Dante Rinaldi, and I love you like I've never loved anyone else. My new vow comes from God's Word: 'Whither thou goest, I will go; and where thou lodgest, I will lodge: thy people shall be my people, and thy God my God: Where thou diest, will I die, and there will I be buried.'"

Shaking his head in an attempt to comprehend what had just happened, Dante pulled her closer. "I've prayed for this, but it seemed impossible that you'd ever love me."

She laughed. "I prayed for the taxes to be paid on Cottonwood, but I thought that was impossible, too. We should have had more faith in God. His plan was the best of all."

Dante roared with laughter, scooped her up into his arms, and whirled her around. "For a day that started out so awful, it's turned into the best of my life."

She squealed and clutched at his chest. "Be careful, Dante."

He stopped and stared at her. "You mean because of the baby?"

Her eyes grew wide. "How did you know?"

"Martha Thompson told me."

Savannah stiffened in his arms. "What?" she shrieked. "I was waiting for the right moment to tell you. How did Martha know?"

"I had asked Mr. Perkins for something to settle your stomach, and Martha diagnosed your condition when she heard your symptoms." He laughed again. "You forget she's the biggest gossip in town. She knows everything."

Savannah relaxed and smiled. "Are you happy?"

"Happy doesn't start to describe how I feel. I can hardly wait to see what else God has planned for us."

Savannah's arms encircled his neck and pulled his head down to meet hers. "Me, too."

nineteen

Savannah sat by the window in the parlor of her and Dante's new home and let her gaze travel over the bare branches of the trees, swaying in the December breeze. Christmas was just a few weeks away, and this year she and Dante had a lot to celebrate.

She leaned back in the rocker Dante had bought her and smiled in satisfaction. Her left foot gently rocked the cradle beside her as she thought of the crocks of newly churned butter sitting on a table in the kitchen. She enjoyed the early afternoon when her chores were complete and her child napped beside her.

It seemed impossible that so much had happened in the last year. Sometimes she had to pinch herself to make sure she hadn't dreamed it all. When she looked into the faces of her husband and child, though, she knew it was all true.

Dante appeared at the corner of the house and bounded onto the front porch. He burst through the door and smiled when he saw her. "I thought I'd come check on you."

Without breaking the rhythm of the cradle, she tilted her head and arched an eyebrow. "You're never going to finish that fence if you keep coming home."

He laughed, walked to the cradle, and gazed down at the baby. "For some reason, I just can't stay away."

Her foot stilled, and she hesitated at the question that had hovered on her lips since the baby's birth. She inhaled. "Dante, are you sorry she isn't a boy?"

A big smile covered his face. "A boy? We can have one of those next. Right now I'm happy to have the two most beautiful women in the world in my life."

She laughed. "You do act like she's kind of special."

He dropped to his knees and trailed a finger across their daughter's head. "Amelia Gabriella Rinaldi, you are a beauty."

Savannah smiled. She never tired of seeing Dante with the daughter they'd named after their mothers. She glanced out the window and squinted to get a better view of the person walking toward their house.

"Dante, someone's coming."

He stood and looked out the window. "I can't tell who it is."

"Neither can I, but it looks. . ." She squealed in happiness. "Dante, it's Jasper. He's come home."

They rushed to the door and stepped onto the porch. Dante stood with his arm around her shoulders as Jasper trudged toward them. When he reached the house, Savannah ran down the steps and embraced him.

Tears ran down her face. "Jasper, I'm so glad to see you."

"Good to see you, too, Miss 'Vanna."

Dante followed her and stuck out his hand. "We didn't think we'd ever see you again."

Jasper grabbed Dante's hand and shook it. "Yas suh, I reckon I thought I never would see ya'll, neither."

"What brought you back?" Savannah asked.

Jasper took off the hat Savannah had seen him wear for years and wiped his brow. "Well, I al'ays wanted to see the ocean, and I seen it. Even slept on the beach for a while just a-lis'nin' to the waves roll in. It shore is a purty sight to see."

Dante nodded. "I lived near it all my life. It's hard to understand how big it is until you see it up close."

Jasper chuckled. "You right about that. But it ain't the

Alabama." He gazed over his shoulder toward the bluff. "I reckon there just ain't no water on God's earth like the river I been knowin' all my life, and I wanted to come back. Mistuh Dante done tole me 'fore I left I always have a home at Cottonwood."

Savannah laughed. "You'll always have a home with us, Jasper."

"Thank you kindly, Miss 'Vanna. It's good to be home."

Savannah and Dante watched as Jasper turned and walked toward the river bluff. Dante looped his arm around Savannah's waist. "The Alabama River brought me to Cottonwood, and the best things of my life happened because of it. I don't ever want to leave it either."

Savannah's heart burst with happiness. She kissed her husband on the cheek and glanced over her shoulder at the first wing of their house that had risen from the ruins of her childhood home. Soon they would begin building the next section, and the big columns would stand once again on the riverbank.

"I'm glad the river brought you here, too. Aunt Jane told me that the only reason to marry was because you loved somebody so much you hurt from wanting to be with them."

Dante's lips brushed the top of her head. "What else did she tell you?"

She snuggled closer to her husband. Memories of the war, worries over unpaid taxes, and threats from murdering gangs vanished in his protective embrace. "That God had great things waiting for me. And you know what, Dante?"

"What?"

Savannah stood on her tiptoes and pulled his head down until their lips almost touched. "She was right."

A Letter To Our Readers

Dear Reader:

In order that we might better contribute to your reading enjoyment, we would appreciate your taking a few minutes to respond to the following questions. We welcome your comments and read each form and letter we receive. When completed, please return to the following:

Fiction Editor
Heartsong Presents
PO Box 719
Uhrichsville, Ohio 44683

1. Did you enjoy reading *The Columns of Cottonwood* by Sandra Robbins?
   ❑ Very much! I would like to see more books by this author!
   ❑ Moderately. I would have enjoyed it more if

   _____

   _____

   _____

2. Are you a member of **Heartsong Presents**? ❑ Yes ❑ No
   If no, where did you purchase this book?_____

   _____

3. How would you rate, on a scale from 1 (poor) to 5 (superior), the cover design? _____

4. On a scale from 1 (poor) to 10 (superior), please rate the following elements.

   ____ Heroine   ____ Plot
   ____ Hero   ____ Inspirational theme
   ____ Setting   ____ Secondary characters

5. These characters were special because? _____

_____

_____

6. How has this book inspired your life? _____

_____

_____

7. What settings would you like to see covered in future
   Heartsong Presents books? _____

_____

_____

8. What are some inspirational themes you would like to see
   treated in future books? _____

_____

_____

9. Would you be interested in reading other **Heartsong
   Presents** titles? ❑ Yes ❑ No

10. Please check your age range:
   ❑ Under 18   ❑ 18-24
   ❑ 25-34   ❑ 35-45
   ❑ 46-55   ❑ Over 55

Name _____

Occupation _____

Address _____

City, State, Zip _____

E-mail _____

SEASIDE ROMANCE

3 stories in 1

Finding their true love requires daring leaps of faith for each of three women from Rhode Island's seaside communities of old.

Historical, paperback, 352 pages, 5³⁄₁₆" x 8"